THE GODS OF OAKLEIGH

JUANITA KEES

THE GODS OF OAKLEIGH

JUANITA KEES

THE GODS OF OAKLEIGH
(previously published as Finding Paradise)

Published by Juanita Kees (Kees2Create)
ISBN Paperback: 978-0-6484995-6-5
ISBN eBook: 978-0-6484995-7-2
ISBN Large Print: 978-0-6484995-8-9

ACKNOWLEDGMENTS

A special thank you to all who support me on this crazy, rollercoaster journey. Readers, authors, family, and friends; without you my dreams could not become reality.

NOTE FROM THE AUTHOR

Thank you so much for taking the time to read *The Gods of Oakleigh.* As the story is set mostly in Australia, I have used Australian English for the text. I hope you will forgive the minor spelling differences between US and UK English to enjoy this fantasy romance.

Please note that this book was previously published as *Finding Paradise.* If you have read it before, I hope you enjoy the new look Greek gods.

All reviews are appreciated.

Best wishes

Juanita Kees

DEDICATION

For my lovely friend, Efthalia, without whose input my Greek Mythology and language would be totally muddled. Pollí agápi, koukla.

ABOUT THE BOOK

The quiet suburb of Oakleigh may never be the same again. Not as long as the gods are in town ...

"Juanita Kees delivers a wonderful twist on the Battle of Troy with this story that starts on Mykonos and moves to modern Melbourne, with a little detour to Paradise on the side. Anything with swords and shields and gorgeous Greek gods will get my attention, plus this one had football and a Twitter meltdown by social media-phobic Zeus himself. I loved it." ~ ***Lily Malone, author, The Vineyard in the Hills***.

"A fresh twist and a sexy modern romance. Enjoyed every page." ~ ***Jennie Jones, author, A Place to Stay***

PROLOGUE

"There are no binding oaths between lions and men,"
~ Achilles to Hector at the Battle of Troy

CIRCA 1250 B.C.

How dare they insult him — Ajax the Great — warrior, defender of the Greeks? How could those swine award the Shield of Achilles to Odysseus after all he'd achieved for them? How dare they disgrace him in such a manner?

Had he not slain twenty-eight Trojans for the Greeks, held off the attacking army single-handedly so Odysseus could remove Achilles' body from the battlefield and lay him to rest beside Patroclus? Had he not taken on Hector — again — and saved the Greek warships from burning? He swallowed a gulp of ambrosia from his goblet, feeling the bite of fermentation in his throat.

Were it not for his size and strength, all would be lost.

All Odysseus had left was the power of charm and the mouth of the devil. He'd believed his deed honourable and deserving, had sold his case to the court and won the Shield of Achilles — with his words, not with his fighting skills. Ajax spat the distaste from his mouth.

Agamemnon and Menelaus, the sons of Atreus, deserved to die for awarding the armour to the man he had once considered a great warrior. No more. Odysseus had betrayed more than loyalty. He'd betrayed their kinship. Vengeance would be his.

"Such murderous thoughts, Ajax the Great, but you are correct. The armour should be yours." Her voice, sweet and coaxing, her words almost believable — had Ajax not known her for the deceitful vixen she was.

"So say you. Yet, are you not Odysseus' greatest admirer? You ... Athena — Goddess of Wisdom — admire his abilities to be well-spoken, his loyalty to his kin and the gods, his bravery and wisdom." Bitterness gave his tone a biting edge.

Athena smiled, cold and calculating. "Ah, but this is different. For once, I believe Odysseus is truly not deserving of his prize. There is a way to redeem your honour." She leaned towards him, her perfume enveloping his senses, her delectable breasts teasing his chest and muddling his thoughts.

He knew Athena was a temptress, a goddess not to be trusted, yet Ajax felt himself falling under her spell as her lips teased his.

"Down in the field they wait for you — Odysseus, Agamemnon and Menelaus — among the cows and sheep they stole from the Trojans. They're drunk on their success and ambrosia, vulnerable in their weakened state." Her clever hands traced the muscles in his arms, working their way across the solid wall of his chest. "You could easily take their lives tonight, for you are Ajax the Great, all-powerful, almighty warrior."

Ajax's mind clouded, the edges of his sanity fading as she coaxed open his lips and breathed the words into his mouth.

"Yes, I am a great warrior," he replied, floating on a cloud of desire and intoxication.

He reached for her, but she danced away. "Then kill them tonight."

The sun burned against his eyelids and raucous laughter surrounded him. Ajax shifted as the grass beneath him chafed his back. He'd killed his adversaries. Slaughtered them, hacked and slashed as they'd bleated for him to spare their lives. The anger surged within him again and he pushed himself up. Where were they — the bodies?

The coppery smell of blood filled his nostrils, as did the stench of something else. Yes, he'd ripped out their hearts and stomachs, covered himself in their blood, wore it now like a symbol of honour of the great warrior he was.

He shook the fog from his mind and opened his eyes. Around him the laughter grew. The Greek army surrounded him, pointing at him and the scene at his feet. They cried out, teasing him, taunting him with cruel words.

"Why are you laughing?" He stood and looked at where they pointed.

Before him, he beheld the mass slaughter of cattle and

sheep. His sword — the gift he'd received from Hector so long ago — laid buried deep between the ribs of a ram, in direct line with its heart.

Athena. She had done this to him, driven him to commit this crime against the people he served. Shame warred with relief. At least he had not murdered his fellow Greeks, instead he had diminished his honour further by slaughtering the spoils of war. He'd be forced to explain his actions to Atreus, to Zeus whom he feared even more. How could he explain the jealous reasons he'd wanted to kill Odysseus and the Achaean leaders? In the harsh light of day and sobriety, all he saw was the senseless destruction he'd wrought. Zeus would banish him. He'd lose his honour among warriors, be deemed unstable and a traitor to his people.

"What possessed you to wreak such havoc upon the field?" Odysseus grabbed his shoulders and spun him around. "Explain yourself. Are you such a selfish bastard that you take out your anger on defenceless animals? Why did you not seek out a more worthy adversary? I would gladly take a sword to you myself instead of this ... massacre.

Ajax covered his face with his blood-spattered hands. The foul smell of decomposing stomach contents reached in and curdled his gut. He retched, shook his head as the taunts around him grew louder. Humiliation, so deep it ripped at his heart, flooded his mind and body. He'd rather die than face degradation.

"Go," shouted Odysseus, raw anger on his face and disgust in his voice. He spat at Ajax's feet. "No doubt Zeus will decide your punishment." Odysseus turned his back and shouted orders for the carcasses to be placed upon a pyre.

Ajax walked towards the body of the ram and retrieved the sword from its heart. In his dream, the ram was Odysseus. The horror of what he'd done — what he could have done — weighed so heavily on his shoulders, they sagged under the pressure and curved his back. A broken warrior, he dragged his feet across the field away from the mayhem, jeers at his back and the sting of stones bouncing off his scalp. He smelled the acrid smoke of his killing spree on the pyre.

Up the hill, he buried the hilt of his sword in the ground and watched the sun glint off the sharp blade. He sat on a pile of rocks and contemplated the punishment his actions would bring. Facing the wrath of Atreus would be humiliating enough, but admitting his guilt to Zeus … not even Ajax the Great was brave enough for that. He had little choice. There was only one solution.

Standing, he towered above the point of his sword. "Forgive me, Zeus. I have disgraced you. My greed and jealousy devoured my humility. I do not deserve your pardon. Instead, I sacrifice myself in the name of honour and leave this earth."

Athena's laughter echoed around him, her voice tormenting him. "Coward."

The word reached into his soul, shattered his heart. "You betrayed me, humiliated and drugged me. May the wrath of Zeus rest upon your shoulders, Athena, for so help me, I will never trust a woman again."

Ajax the Great closed his eyes, took a steadying breath and fell on his sword. He felt the burn as the blade pierced his side, heard the rip as it sliced his flesh, bore the moment of pain as it reached his heart and then mercifully, his world went black.

Odysseus rattled the gates of hell. “Come out and explain yourself, Ajax. Did owning the Shield of Achilles really mean more to you than your life, the lives of others? Surely the warrior in you can see that it is not the shield that makes the man, but rather the man himself?”

Silence met his plea. Nothing but heat and cries of torment passed through the blackened gates. Where in hell was Ajax? Zeus refused to talk about the misadventure. In fact, the great god of gods refused to speak his name at all, so fierce was his anger at Ajax’s suicide. It would take Zeus a while to reign in the fury, which he lashed out on the seas, creating magnificent storms and waves so high they dwarfed the ships upon them.

Odysseus called Ajax’s name over and over until Hades himself stepped from the flames. “Do be quiet, Odysseus. Your constant bawling sets my horns afire. Ajax isn’t here. His soul is trapped in the darkness between hell and Earth. The last I heard, he was wandering aimlessly in Erebus. For some ungodly reason, Zeus spared him the sentence of being sent straight to hell. Damn shame, really. I could use him down here. All these thieves, murderers, Romans — it’s like trying to control a room full of adolescents, I tell you.”

“Don’t bother me with your strife, Hades. How can I reach Ajax?”

Hades stroked his pointy beard, his hands gnarled, nails blackened with ash. He shrugged. “You can’t. Not without Zeus' permission. Zeus has sentenced him to two thousand years in Erebus to consider his sins. No-one is to make contact with him in that time, not even I. Word is, he is on the island of Leuke at the mouth of the Danube, guarding the sanctuary containing the remains of Achilles and Patroclus from the scourge of the seas. Damn pirates. No doubt someday they'll end up down here too. I hope he doesn't learn his lesson. I won't give up until I have his soul."

Odysseus sighed. There was nothing he could do but wait.

CHAPTER ONE

MODERN DAY MELBOURNE

Ajax wandered the banks of the Yarra. When everyone on Olympus thought Zeus had sent him to the island of Leuke, he'd arrived in Van Diemen's Land, and then travelled to a place so hot he'd have preferred hell.

For over two thousand years he'd watched Australia grow from a barren wasteland to a bustling metropolis. He'd wandered from coast to coast, seeking peace for his soul. He'd crossed deserts Hades would think suitable for new settlements, witnessed the arrival of the first boats to the shores — the men and women with their chocolate-coloured skin and tribal ways. Then later, the arrival of the others and the discordance it had brought upon the land. Two world wars, the depression of the 1930s, terror attacks, and now, finally, a form of unsettled peace as if the world still sat on the edge of its seat waiting for something to happen … just like him.

"Ah, Ajax," said Zeus, touching his shoulder. "I've been looking all over for you. I have a job for you to do."

Ajax sighed. Another test, another failure. He touched the scar on his side. Every time Zeus set him a task, the damn thing itched like buggery, reminding him of his cowardice, selfishness and greed.

"Of course," he agreed, turning to the great god.

Sometimes he wished Zeus would just give up and let him die, send him to hell for Hades to play with. That's what a coward deserved, after all. But no, instead Zeus played his own game of cat and mouse.

"I'm sending you to Paradise Beach, Mykonos, on protection detail. Arianrhod, the future Queen of the Faeries, is holidaying there and I fear Hades is looking for trouble with her. He's been chasing control of her queendom for years. I need you to keep her out of his way until I figure out a way of getting her onto the throne. He's a charming devil and before you know it, he'll have control of Paradise."

Ajax shook his head. "A woman? You want me to protect a woman? Zeus, you know how I feel about those creatures. They're traitorous, conniving hellions. No, I'm sorry. I'd rather you just finish me now." Pain sliced his heart as sure as the blade of his sword had. Athena's betrayal had struck deep. He'd kept his promise for centuries — millennium even — never to trust a woman again. He sure as hell had no desire to play bodyguard to one.

"I'm afraid you have no choice, my boy."

"There's always a choice, Zeus."

"Oh come now, Ajax. Are you saying you'll abandon your friends in their time of need too? I know you think you're a coward for what you did all those years ago, but are you one to desert your friends seeking their own way out of Purgatory?"

Ajax frowned. Odysseus and Helen? God knows, he knew all about their struggles too. Suspicion crawled up his spine. What the hell was Zeus playing at?

"You're using my friends as a bargaining tool to get me to protect a Faerie Queen and sending me to one of the most beautiful beaches in the world to do it." He shook his head. "There has to be a catch."

Zeus shrugged. "Well, I figured you're all due for a little visit to the homeland so why not kill two harpies with one stone, so to speak. Not that I'd ever harm my harpies, of course."

"Of course," Jax agreed dryly.

Not even the harpies escaped Zeus' tests unscathed. Olympus was littered with their feathers, singed from being put through their paces at training. No point arguing with the great god, he'd only lose the battle … again.

Jax sighed. "What is it you want from me?"

Zeus patted his shoulder. "I knew you'd see it my way. Young Arianrhod is unaware that she is the Queen of Paradise. You see, her grandmother died without handing over the reign or telling her granddaughter of the queendom she'd inherit. Hades has been wreaking havoc up there in the absence of a leader, turning the faeries to the dark side, destroying vegetation and food sources to force them to follow him. I need you to stop him claiming Paradise."

Ajax snorted, anger simmering in his belly. "You want

me to stop Hades on a path of destruction and convince some empty-headed young thing she's a Faerie Queen? Clearly you have not had any dealings with Generation Y. You cannot tell them anything." He turned his attention to the choppy waters of the Yarra. Best he reined in his temper or the rowing team from Melbourne Boys Grammar School would end up head first in the freezing water. He closed his eyes and focused on easing his fury and gentling the waves. Only when they'd settled did he speak. "I couldn't win an argument over the Shield of Achilles yet you want me to win a war against the devil. Have you changed the strength of your ambrosia?"

Zeus chuckled. "Souping up the ambrosia … there's an idea. What is more important to you, Ajax? A piece of armour or good deed that might save the world? But yes, putting Hades in his place is precisely what I want, and I believe you're the man for the job."

How many times had Zeus said those same words to him? *You can do it, Ajax. I believe in you. If anyone can do it, you can.* And he'd failed every task assigned to him for over two thousand years because he was a coward and his own self-hate had eaten away his heart, leaving him empty and alone.

"If I fail this task, will you leave me be and let my soul rest?"

Zeus cocked an eyebrow and laughed so loud the cox in the boat startled, overbalanced and fell in the water. "If you fail this test, dear boy, you and I both may as well knock on the gates of hell and beg to be let in." He turned to walk away, throwing his parting words over his shoulder. "Helen has your passport and tickets. You leave in the morning via this cursed new-world transport they call an airplane. Nice work on not toppling that boat, by the way. Two thousand years ago you would have dumped them in the water for the mere pleasure of it. You've come further than you think, Ajax the Great."

Ajax doubted it. If he had, then why did he feel so goddamn worthless? "Zeus, how will I find her?" he called out to Zeus' retreating back.

Zeus waved his hand in the air, but didn't look around. "Don't worry, she'll find you."

Paradise Beach, Mykonos

"It's not that there's anything wrong with men, Penny," Arian Kendrick told her best friend as they sipped cocktails under an umbrella on the stretch of white sand. "I want more from a relationship than football and meat pies on a Saturday. I want to be loved, respected and treated as an equal partner, not a door prize."

"The football world adored you." Her friend sighed.

Arian laughed, the sound dry in her throat. "No, they didn't. They adored the person they saw at red carpet presentations in designer gowns and torturous heels, reporters aiming their cameras at necklines waiting for boobs to fall out of stick-on bras and make the evening news."

And when *exactly that* had happened, hadn't she suffered the humiliation for months? Belittled by fashionistas, ridiculed by the WAGs and stalked by the press, they'd whittled away at her confidence and destroyed her pride. Suddenly she had the most famous nipples worldwide for all the wrong reasons, and the disgrace was all her own.

Penny snorted. "Not your fault. You know it was Merlene and her band of merry bitches that instigated your wardrobe fail. Payback because she wanted Craig and he only had eyes for you."

"Well, she got him. It worked. Hope she's happy."

The coach's daughter always got what she wanted, and she could have Craig McMahon. Arian was done being latched onto the arm of a man who'd rather be kicking a ball around and sleeping his way to success than take a relationship seriously.

She'd never been part of Merlene's snooty purple circle, nor did she aspire to be. Thankfully not all the WAGS had been that vicious and she had made friends — like Penny.

"Someday, Penny, I'm going to meet a man who appreciates me for who I am. A man who is proud of my career, respects me as a businesswoman and doesn't need a trophy wife but a life partner."

Her pride still throbbed from the digs the press had made. That surely she wasn't smart enough to be a geographical surveyor, and she really should settle down into a housewife-gym routine if she was serious about Craig McMahon and supporting his career.

Arian sat back and took a long slug of her Fluffy Duck cocktail while Penny pondered on her words.

For two years, she'd played down her passion for her own career to take on the glittery role of the footballer's girlfriend because she'd truly believed she loved him, that he could fill that empty space in her heart and be The One for her.

Yet throughout the duration of their relationship, the feeling of not belonging had dogged her. Deep in her heart she'd known she was too grounded to walk the red carpet and grace the football stadium's VIP boxes forever.

Annoyed and frustrated by the hollowness of their relationship, and realising the only one he would ever truly love was himself, she'd left the great Craig McMahon, Melbourne's favourite football son.

But it wasn't just Craig's world where she didn't feel comfortable any longer. Ever since Gran died, she'd felt she didn't belong anywhere, like a soul lost in the universe waiting to be given direction.

"Mmm, good men like that are harder to uncover than vestal virgins," mused Penny. "You'll need to kiss a lot of frogs first."

Arian smiled. "I think I've kissed my last footballer, that's for sure. I don't have the patience for all the politics and bitchiness behind the scenes in the football world."

"Yep, 'all that glitters is not gold' and all that crap," Penny agreed. "So you don't want another football star and you're not looking for a run-of-the-mill Aussie bloke either ... you do know they rate third in the world in penis size, right?"

Arian choked on a mouthful of liquid. "Jesus, Penny, where do you find these jewels of information?"

Penny shrugged. "It's amazing what you can find out online. Just because my Simon and your Craig turned out to be dickheads, doesn't mean all guys are like that."

Arian tipped her sunglasses up to study the rapidly disappearing, thick yellow liquid in her glass. "He didn't start out as one. There was a time when he was a nice guy. Pity his ego grew too big in the end."

"Oh well, at least he was good in bed, right? And he had a bloody nice arse — all tight and toned. Be honest, you knew the relationship wouldn't last. Too many groupies following him around, wheedling their way into his hotel room. While we're on the subject of lads and layabouts, who would you consider your ideal man?"

"I don't know … maybe someone who is kind, romantic and adventurous. Someone who will be there for me, pick me up when I'm down, celebrate my achievements with me. A man who doesn't mind cuddling after sex instead of flipping over and turning the telly on. Someone who appreciates I have a brain in my head and not a pinch of silicone anywhere. And I lied about Craig being good in bed. He was a lousy, selfish lover who ran on adrenaline and very little else."

No matter how hard she'd tried, nothing could reignite the flame between them, not when Craig had already moved on. Now she had to do the same. Was it so wrong to want a relationship that *wasn't* one-sided? Was it asking for miracles that she find a life partner who shared the same passion she did, that the chemistry between them would strengthen, develop, and evolve into something deeper and eternal?

Arian waved a hand across her knees at the brilliant blue sea in front of their sun-loungers. "Greece is meant to be the land of the gods, right? Where are the men of honour, the warriors of the past? Those mythical beings that craved adventure and enjoyed a good fight, yet they knew how to love a woman."

"That's why they're myths, hon. They never existed. And don't believe all that crap Craig and the media put into your head. You're a lovely, kind-hearted, clever girl and a great friend. That arsehole wouldn't know a good thing if it hit him in the back of the head." Penny studied the horizon. "Speaking of Greek gods and myths, check it out ..."

Arian dragged her gaze from her glass and dropped her sunglasses back down on her nose. Following the direction of Penny's nod, she watched a man rise from the roll of waves slapping against the sand. Even from up the beach, she could tell he was tall. He dwarfed the swimmers around him, turned heads as he loped up the beach on long, strong, shapely legs. Hair dark and sleeked back with water, he was undeniably sexy with his rich bronze skin and ripped physique. She could easily imagine him as a Greek warrior, with and without his *chitoniskos*.

A spark of attraction caught her off guard as it bounced off her heart and knotted in her stomach. There was something about him … something oddly familiar … as if she knew him or should know him. Impossible, he was very definitely Mediterranean heritage and this was her first trip anywhere near the islands. She shook off the *deja vu*.

"Married," she said, waving a hand at where he sprinted up the sand to swoop a giggling little girl onto his hip and slip an arm around an equally gorgeous woman in what barely passed as a bikini.

"Maybe not. She could be his sister." Penny scanned the horizon again. "Ah well, I'm sure the right one is out there somewhere. He'll come along when the time is right."

"I guess." Arian watched as the god from the sea sat down on the sand and began building a sandcastle, much to the delight of the little girl who promptly stamped a chubby foot on the north-side wall. He tickled her toes and chased after her as she ran away up the beach towards them.

"Incoming," warned Penny, and Arian barely had a moment to snatch her drink out of the way.

The little girl skidded to a halt beside her and popped her thumb in her mouth. "*Kalispera,*" she said with a lisp.

"Hi there," responded Arian as she propped herself up on her elbows.

"*O theios mou* ..." She looked like a little doll with big blue eyes and blonde curls as she waved a plump little arm towards the man-god coming up the beach, his pace slower now.

"Is that your daddy?" Arian asked.

"I think *theios* means uncle. Either way, we're about to find out," Penny responded, watching the man head towards them. She blew out a breath on a whistle. "Holy hotness, Arian ..." Penny's whisper tapered off as a shadow loomed over them.

If Arian thought he was sexy rising from the sea, he was goddamn chilli-hot up close. Eyes as blue as the sea behind him, hair curling comfortably at his nape and a body that cried out for caressing, the title Man-god did not do him justice.

"*Sygnomi, kyria.*" His voice swept down her spine and enveloped her like a dark velvet shroud, making her toes curl and her body tingle with pleasure.

"Hi," Arian breathed, ignoring Penny's snort.

Blue eyes burned into hers, turning the tingle into a delicious shiver. Arian tipped her sunglasses up on her head and dismissed his gaze. No way would she fall for a pair of sexy eyes again. The last pair she'd fallen in love with had hidden a mean, selfish personality.

Entranced despite her determination to ignore him, she watched his large, long-fingered hand stroke the soft brown beard across his jawline. Yes, no matter how sexy he was — even with a beard — she *so* was *not* interested. At least, not until he proved he was capable of holding a conversation without inviting her to warm his bed like Craig had. Craig had believed he could achieve world peace just by having sex.

Since Man-god was here in all his glory though, she might as well enjoy the view. He dropped his hand to his side, and she allowed her gaze to follow it to where she was forced to appreciate the snug fit of the bathers clinging to his hips. *Dear Lord.* Her eyes snapped back to his. Damned if Penny's theory about long fingers and big hands wasn't true … if she cared, which she didn't, so it didn't matter.

His raised eyebrow and cold look challenged her. Heat that had nothing to do with the sun flushed her face. She swallowed her embarrassment. So she'd looked … so what? If he didn't want to be ogled he should have worn board shorts that would have concealed his attributes instead of showing them off.

Eyes still fixed on hers, he held out a hand to the little girl. "*Ela,* Ermioni." With a mock salute, he turned and walked away.

For a moment, the girls admired the rear view as he swung the little girl into his arms and walked back towards the water. Penny licked her thumb, pressed it against her shoulder and made a hissing sound.

"Phwoar, that man is H.O.T." She tipped her glass in a

toast to the threesome who now sat on the sand with the little girl playing at their feet.

"Well … hell," said Arian, a little miffed at the look of scorn he'd given her before he'd walked away.

He'd made her feel like a tart and she was damn sure he'd felt like a piece of meat, the way she'd eyed him off. Sure, that had been her intention at first, but then she'd seen that flicker of hurt and betrayal in his eyes. It intrigued and confused her. Most men — especially those with honed bodies like his — preened as they paraded the beach when admired by women. Man-god had looked disgusted, even a little uncomfortable.

Looking down the beach from her sun lounger, Arian studied the tableau the family set. The couple sat close together, their heads almost touching as they shared a secret, so engrossed in each other they didn't see the little girl get up and wander towards the water. Arian watched as she paddled happily in the shallows with the waves lapping at her little ankles.

She envied the family their bond, their happiness and their beautiful child. Craig had never wanted kids, another reason she'd known in the end he wasn't the man for her. If she ever found the man of her dreams, he would adore his children, be a good father and a loving, attentive husband, just like the man on the beach. All the things she hadn't had with Craig.

The little girl bent down to cup water in her palms then threw her arms wide, giggling as the water splashed through her fingers. Arian's smile turned to horror as a freak wave curled fast and furiously across the sea towards the shore, gathering speed until it swept the little girl up onto the crest and swallowed her as it tumbled and broke.

Arian didn't think twice as she screamed, "Hey, look out."

She ran past the stunned couple who'd rushed to their feet, and didn't stop until she was waist high in the water. She searched around her and saw nothing. Taking a deep breath, she plunged below the surface, saltwater stinging her eyes as she peered into the depths. The water, so clear and blue from the beach, was dark and murky here, making it difficult to see.

Her heart pounded in her chest and an ache formed in her throat. Where was the little girl? What if she was too late? Like she'd been too late for … no, she would *not* think of that now. This was another time, another life at risk and she'd be damned if she'd let the sea take another victim.

She rose to the surface to take a gasp of air. Man-god was in the water now too. What the hell was the matter with him? He just stood there, frozen as the sea ebbed and flowed around him. Why wasn't he diving, looking for his little girl? She wanted to shout at him to help her, but the words caught in her throat. Every minute wasted meant a step closer to death for the little girl. Fear and urgency mingled in her chest. Never again did she want to see the bloated, blue-lipped appearance of a drowning victim, especially not another child.

Shrugging off the feeling of impending doom, Arian dived again, deeper this time. Seaweed floated in the current like dark eerie hands reaching out, touching and capturing creatures of the sea. Agitation clawed at her stomach as she swam towards the rocks resting on the seabed. She had no idea where she was or how far from shore she'd swum. All she knew was a desperate need to find the little girl before it was too late.

Something black loomed before her, baring its teeth. Evil vibrated off the pitch-black shadow. Her lungs screamed for oxygen as she struggled not to open her mouth and cry out. Clutched in the monster's grip was the little girl, her body limp. Ghoulish red eyes peered at her through the murky water, but Arian focused on the precious bundle in its hold. Her vision darkened and eerie voices echoed in her head. Hatred pulled at her heart, but she refused to let it in. She pushed away the thoughts and feelings, and silently chanted the version of St Patrick's Prayer her grandmother had taught her when she'd been younger and afraid of the dark.

I bind unto myself today
The virtues of the starlit heavens,
The glorious sun's life-giving ray,
The whiteness of the moon at even,
The flashing of the lightning free,
The whirling wind's tempestuous shocks,
The stable earth, the deep salt sea,
Around the old eternal rocks,
So may it be.

With a roar of pain, the looming black shadow retreated, hands clutching its head, and the little girl floated free. Arian reached for her, clasped her to her chest and kicked up towards the surface.

Strong hands reached for her as she broke through, gasping for air. Ignoring the grasp of support and kicking to stay afloat, she turned the little girl on her back and rested the curly head against her. Desperately, she breathed long breaths into the mouth that not so long ago had smiled and laughed on the shore.

Arian felt herself dragged back against the man's chest, his arms supported her and she thanked the gods he was strong enough to drag them both ashore. In the shallows, she found her footing and despite the burning in her lungs, continued to breathe life into the little girl.

Reaching the sand, she sank to her knees and lay the girl down to begin CPR.

"*Kyria,* let me help with Ermioni," he said, as Arian alternated between palpitating the tiny heart with two fingers and breathing past the blue lips into Ermioni's mouth.

Ermioni, what a beautiful name, she thought, and let him take over the breathing. Her heart ached, her head pounded and her muscles screamed, but she couldn't give up. She murmured the same blessing over and over in her mind until, with a sharp cough, the girl vomited water.

"Thank you, thank you," she whispered, tears stinging her eyes as she rolled the little girl into recovery position and stroked her curly head.

As soon as Ermioni stopped retching and breathed freely again, her mother swept her up in her arms, crying her name over and over. Man-god placed a hand on Arian's shoulder. She shook it off. She wanted to shout at him, scream for an answer as to why he'd just stood there while his little girl was drowning, just as her father had when Timmy … The little girl was crying now, she was alive. That's all that mattered. There could be a million reasons for his actions and none of them were her business. She shook off her anger at him as he spoke.

"*Sas efcharisto, kyria.* Without you, my niece would be gone. I am in your debt."

Arian shook her head then regretted the movement as pain pounded her skull. "She's safe. She's okay."

That the little girl had lived was thanks enough, but what the hell was that down there? What had she seen? Those red eyes filled with evil haunted her mind. Who would believe her if she told them?

Ajax ruffled little Ermioni's fair curls, then turned back to the woman who'd rescued her. "Are you alright?"

One didn't spend some two thousand years avoiding the likes of Hades and not get to know his smell, his presence. He'd felt that evil in the swell and hadn't even tried to fight against it. The force with which Hades had held him back had left him weak and dizzy. How had this woman survived? Hades was merciless and she a mere human, yet he'd let her and Ermioni live. At least for now, he reminded himself. What was the damn devil trying to prove?

"I'm okay, thank you. I'm glad I got to her in time." She avoided his eyes, but he didn't miss the flicker of fear there.

"I do not have enough words to thank you, *kyria*."

She bent and clasped her knees, shaking a little.

"Can I get you anything?" He tried again.

The woman shook her head. Earlier, when he'd met her on the beach, she'd been relaxed, glowing and even a little smug, but now her face grew grey and haunted. "No, no, thank you."

"Please, let us take you to a doctor. It is the least we can do to show our gratitude." No matter how much she'd angered him earlier with her lustful perusal of his body, he could forgive her now — for Ermioni and Helen's sakes.

The woman raised a hand to her head as if it hurt to keep upright. "That's very kind of you but no, thank you. I … I need to go … to my room."

In a flash, her friend was there, her arm around the woman's shoulders. "I'm glad your little girl is safe, but Arian needs rest. She's had quite a shock."

Arian? Could this be the Faerie Queen? The one he was meant to protect? "Yes, yes, of course, I understand." Disappointment flooded him. He'd failed his first test. He hadn't protected her or Ermioni from Hades, hadn't even realised who she was.

He watched as the two women stopped to say something to Helen, who reached out and kissed their cheeks. Then they were walking away and an emptiness filled Jax's heart and mind far worse than any he'd felt in two thousand years. All this time and still he was a coward.

"You are not a coward, Ajax the Great. You could not have saved Ermioni from Hades. She was bait." Helen touched his arm. "It's you he wants. He would have taken them to hell, knowing you'd follow."

"How could I have followed when I'd frozen like the coward I am? Again, I am a failure. I'd rather he take me and end this nonsense."

"No, Zeus has given you a second chance and you should take that. No-one blamed you for what happened after Troy. Athena is to blame for intoxicating you and scrambling your mind. Zeus has dealt with her as she deserves."

"Why then did the entire army laugh at me?" The pain and humiliation of his misdeeds resurfaced. "Odysseus spat at my feet. I am a coward not worthy of his friendship, not even after two thousand years. I stood and watched today while Ermioni nearly drowned. I feared Hades so much I could not save her life."

"Your powers are weakened and he took advantage of that. Ermioni is alive. Someone did save her, someone who has powers to resist his evil. Who is she, Ajax?"

"My next test, I believe. Her name is Arianrhod, and she is Queen of Paradise — or at least, she will be soon." Anguish squeezed his heart. If she'd been weaker and unable to resist the evil, Hades would have won the battle for Paradise without even trying too hard.

Helen laid a small, soft hand over his big one. "This is not good, *file mou.* You will need to find a way to protect her … and yourself. She has put herself in danger by saving Ermioni today. I fear Hades will be a challenge to you finding your way out of Purgatory but he is a true and present danger to the queen."

"Yes," he said, quietly accepting his fate. Could this be his redemption? Could he truly protect this woman from the devil? "I think this will be a battle far more challenging than Troy."

"This time you must not fall on your sword. There is a lesson to be learned. That's why Zeus has given you another chance."

"I know and I won't disappoint him again. What about you, my dear friend, Helen of Troy? I wonder why Zeus has brought you back."

Helen shrugged. “Why did he have me cast out as a traitor and adulteress?” Resignation weighed heavily in her tone. Their battle for redemption had only just begun.

They sat on the sand in silence, holding the little girl close between them, a chieftain and a traitor returned to the modern world to seal their fate and right the wrongs of their past.

Hell and damnation. Hades paced the beach on Santorini, cursing his run of bad luck. Who was the *idiot* who’d come between him and his target? Those cursed words she’d conjured had burned right through him, damn it. They’d weakened him in a way he hadn’t been in centuries, not since that damned Welsh Faerie Queen Arianrhod had crossed his path back when the Earth was younger.

Could this be her offspring? Could he accidently have stumbled upon the missing Queen of Paradise? Surely not. Yet she carried the sickening heavenly scent of goodness and purity. If she was the errant ruler, it was bloody inconvenient for her to show up now when he’d only just begun to gain control of her queendom.

This had to be the work of Zeus, always interfering in his bloody plans, exactly as he had when he’d sent Ajax the Great to Earth instead of Paradise. As if changing the name from Paradise to Leuke would make a difference, or hide it from him. Zeus’ attempt at diversion in the wake of the missing queen had failed miserably because he’d found it in the end, extracted the co-ordinates from Arianrhod’s mind before it wasted away along with her body in the curse of mortality — old age.

Eye on the target, he reminded himself. He'd have to find another way. Ajax the Great's soul would be his. Once a coward, always a coward — it was the only way he'd get him through the gates of hell then into the fray to fight for the reign of Paradise. All Hades had to do was make sure the woman didn't cross either of their paths again.

CHAPTER TWO

Music pounded through the Paradise Club as bodies swayed to the rhythm of Greece's latest rock sensation. Filled to capacity, there was no room to breathe. Arian and Penny edged their way out and headed outside away from the crush for the quieter edges of the terrace. Below them, the ocean reflected the light of the full moon as it lapped at the sand.

"How are you feeling?" asked Penny.

"Better. What a shock though. I'm glad I could find her. I don't know, Penny. It was strange. I don't know what I saw, but I tell you, I was damn terrified." Arian shuddered. "I don't want to think about it anymore. I want to forget. That's why we're here, right? To get over Craig and Simon, and to enjoy our freedom for a while." Arian swirled the swizzle stick in her Greek Tiger, then licked the orange juice off it. Far too much juice and far too little ouzo, she thought.

"Well, I'm bloody proud of you, buddy. Do you realise that's the first time you've been in the sea since Timmy's accident?" Penny sucked on the twist of lime from the edge of her glass and took a swig sans the straw. She pulled a face as the bitterness of the lime mixed with the orange juice. "Ugh, that's gross. Can I have your slice of lime?"

The accident … every time she thought about it, it hurt. The years since had not dulled the ache. Regret and what ifs could never bring her little brother back to life. Arian shook off the melancholy and smacked Penny's hand away as she reached across to lift it from the rim of her glass. "No. I thought you said it's gross, so why the hell would you want it? Did you hear what I said?"

"Yeah, yeah. And I like limes, just not with orange juice." Penny waved a careless hand. "So, are we going to have crazy rebound sex with some Greek god and forget about happy-ever-after? At least we'll have memories of Mediterranean hotness."

Arian sighed. "After today, I think I've had enough excitement to last a lifetime. Besides, the only man I could settle for is a god and, as you keep telling me, they're a myth."

"Seriously? You believe that crap?"

"Why wouldn't I? Fairytales were my life until Gran died. She'd always make up stories of how she and I are descendants of the mythical Welsh goddess, Arianrhod, honoured at full moon for her beauty, rumoured to be the Faerie Queen of fertility and reincarnation." Arian sighed. "If only it were true. Paradise sounded ... well, like Paradise, I guess."

"Where is the fun in perfect?" Penny scoffed. "Take a look around you, hon. This is as good as it gets."

The ouzo finally joined the orange juice in the straw

and Arian sucked hard. Her head spun a little as the alcohol soared through her system. "Maybe if it existed, Timmy would still be alive, like Ermioni." Sadness tugged at her heart for a moment. Her dad had never been the same after Timmy drowning. His easy smile had faded and his eyes carried the pain of a man who'd failed his family. "Maybe the perfect man for me only exists in an alternate universe."

Penny grinned. "There's nothing wrong with Aussie men."

"I never said there was. If only all men were like Hugh Jackman, it would be so easy."

"Couldn't agree more, but when have you ever settled for easy? Hey, speaking of superheroes and marriageable men … isn't that Mr Hot down there on the beach? His mate's not too bad either."

Arian allowed her gaze to follow the length of sand below. Her heart skipped a beat as the two men came into view. Man-god from the beach was dressed for clubbing and if the moulded bathers had done him justice, the smooth black pants and navy shirt, unbuttoned and flapping in the gentle breeze, sent him right over the danger point on the Hot-o-Meter. She breathed in the bitterness of ouzo, and choked.

The sting of alcohol burned her throat and sneaked up her nose as she coughed and thrust her drink at Penny. With a hand over her mouth and tears streaming from her eyes, heaving with the effort to breathe, she bent over at the waist.

"Jeez, Arian, are you okay?" Penny patted her back. "Oh my God, you're choking. Help, someone!"

Arian waved a hand at her, trying to catch a breath.

The sound of running on the tiled terrace reached her ears as dizziness threatened to swallow her into blackness. A pair of sandy bare feet appeared in her watery line of vision, followed by strong muscular thighs cling-wrapped in smooth black pants.

Warm fingers wrapped around her chin and lifted her head gently. "Look at me, *kyria*."

Arian obeyed the velvet tones and raised her red-rimmed eyes to his. The impact of his gaze had the same result as a shot of adrenaline, and she found herself sucking in a well-needed breath. With each moment his eyes held hers, the contracted muscles of her throat eased and the sting of alcohol up her nose abated. Warm hands stroked her neck, down across her shoulders, followed the length of her arms to capture her hands.

Much later she would wonder how, why. Now, as the sting flowed through her veins and out her fingertips into his hands, she could only thank God for the fresh air that swirled in her tortured lungs.

"Straighten up now, slowly ..." His deep, accented voice flowed through her with the smoothness of warm chocolate on a fountain. "No, keep your eyes on mine."

Arian stood, swaying a little as the blood that had rushed to her head when she'd bent over drained back into her body. She took a deep breath and released it slowly. "Thank you."

He smiled. "You're welcome. Okay now?"

"Yes, thank you … um … I'm sorry, I didn't catch your name on the beach earlier today?"

"Jax … Jax Polemistis."

His fingers stroked hers with a gentle rhythm and

Arian had trouble remembering her own name. "Arian … Arian Kendrick."

Jax took a small step back and bowed without releasing her hands. "Arianrhod, Faerie Queen and Restorer of Souls. I'm glad I saved yours tonight. We are even, it seems."

Arian's head spun from the contact of his warm palms on hers. "Yes, equal," she rasped, her throat raw from the burn of ouzo. Realising he still held her hands, and aware of the tingling message her reawakened hormones transmitted, she slid her fingers from his. Putting her hands behind her back, away from temptation, she said, "Thank you, Mr Polemistis."

"It's Jax. Stick to the Fluffy Ducks." He picked up the shoes he'd dropped earlier and turned to walk away. "Come, Odys. I need a drink."

The girls watched them retreat. He had a really nice, firm butt, and Arian had felt the muscles in his arms out in the sea today, but she didn't want to think about that. What had her attention was the connection she'd felt when he'd touched her, as if they were bound somehow. The sizzle and pop where their fingertips touched and the tattoo her heart beat against her ribs when she'd looked into his eyes. Did his lips taste good? If she'd kissed him, would he have kissed her back?

Arian, what the hell are you thinking? Time to lay off the ouzo. Clearly it was messing with her mind.

A little way down the terrace, Jax turned his head and looked directly at Arian. *I'll see you around.*

Arian gasped.

Jax raised two fingers to his temple in a mock salute and suddenly Arian had difficulty breathing for another reason altogether. Heat shafted through her as she heard his voice — as clear as day and as sexy as hell — in her mind.

"Oh. My. God. Arian, what the hell happened just there? That was the weirdest bit of first aid I've ever seen. Wow, there were like ... sparks between the two of you."

"I wish I knew. His eyes … he ..." Arian sat down on the cool tiles of the terrace, her shaking legs no longer able to hold her. "He read my mind."

"He what?" Penny sat down beside her.

A cool breeze whipped up around them as Arian willed her hands to stop trembling. "I was thinking what a nice arse he had and I heard his voice in my head telling me he'd see me around."

"Jesus, are you serious? Are you sure someone didn't spike your drink? Maybe with the lack of oxygen —"

Arian shook her head.

Penny stared at her for a long moment. "Okay, after what I saw happen back there, I can believe it. Weird."

"Weird isn't the word I'd use. When he held my hands, I could feel this force pulling at me. The moment I looked into his eyes, my throat opened and I could breathe. I swear I felt that ouzo drain out of my fingertips." She wiggled her fingers to rid them of the tingling sensation that lingered.

"Well, there certainly was a little spark there. Do you think you might be attracted to him?"

Arian thought for a moment. "I'd be lying if I said no, but this was more than attraction. More like a connection."

Penny sighed. "Well, that's not a bad thing then."

"What do you mean?"

"Well, you were too entranced to notice but your Greek

god ...” Penny paused while Arian dropped her hand and focused on her friend’s face. “Judging from his sexy accent, he’s as Melbournian as tzatziki with a little Vegemite on the side.”

“Don’t even think about it, Odysseus.” Down the terrace from where the girls sat, Jax dusted the sand from his feet with his socks.

“Ah, come now. You wouldn’t be scared of a little competition would you, mate?”

He shook his head. “I’m in enough trouble as it is. I don’t need a woman around to complicate things. Surely Zeus could have found me an Earth war to fight instead? I’m a warrior, not a bloody babysitter. For gods’ sakes man, she can’t even handle alcohol.”

After what Athena had done to him, he’d vowed never to fall under a woman’s spell again. No way would he break that vow now, no matter how beautiful Ermioni’s rescuer was or that he’d be spending quite some time protecting her from the devil himself.

Odys chuckled and slapped Jax on the shoulder. “With your weakness for redheads with skin like silk and eyes as green as the grass on Olympus? The chips are down. I give you a week before you fall so hard Hades will wonder what shook the foundations of hell.”

“Well you know where you can put your bets, don’t you? I’ve avoided the so-called love trap for over two thousand years. In all that time I’ve seen nothing but devilry and mischief from womankind. They lure you in, use your body and cast you aside with a stake in your heart. I doubt a Faerie Queen will prove any different."

He pulled on his socks and slipped his feet into his shoes. With nimble fingers he buttoned his shirt, rolling his wide shoulders against the smooth fabric.

Sure he was attracted. When he'd held her in his arms as he'd pulled them to shore, she'd fitted against him like the missing part to the jigsaw puzzle he was. In another lifetime, he wouldn't have hesitated to seduce her and love her so completely she'd forget the real world existed, but this was the here and now. He no longer deserved a good woman or love. Not until he'd found a way to pay his debt to Zeus for being taken by Athena's wiles. And then there was Hades … he'd rather face ten Athenas than walk the path to hell with the devil.

He shrugged off the feeling of foreboding and ignored the sting of sulphur in the air. "Anyway, there is no competition. One dance with me, and she won't know you exist."

Odys smoothed a hand over his curly brown hair and pulled the length of it out of his shirt collar. "Is that a challenge?"

Jax shot him an irritated look. "Everything with you is a challenge. Hands off."

"My friend, remember the last time that jealousy of yours raised its ugly head? It didn't end well. I have no desire to be pulling a sword from your chest again."

"I don't recall asking you to do it the first time. Besides, I think you're fairly safe there since Zeus has it locked up securely in the vault beneath the floor of the house in Oakleigh, along with the Shield of Achilles." Jax rolled down the sleeves of his shirt and buttoned the cuffs. Adjusting his shirt tails, he said grumpily, "I don't want to think about it anymore. I need to replenish my energy. That girl sure packs a punch and I need a drink. Just not ouzo, though. There's enough in my system now to last me a while, and that dose reeked of trouble."

Odys chuckled. "You can't avoid the subject forever, my friend. Sooner or later, you'll have to face up to why you're here."

"Let's make it later, yes?" Jax tilted his head towards the end of the terrace where Arian and Penny walked towards the doors of Paradise Club. "I think we should keep an eye on the two girls tonight. I have a feeling we'll have a battle on our hands before the night's over."

"You're sensing trouble already? Here I thought we were going to have a quiet night for a change." Odys sighed.

Jax shook his head. "There are too many men inside indulging in the spoils of Greece, and the devil is playing bartender. Hades is here. I can smell him. Might explain what happened to Arian's drink. There was more than ouzo in there. If she hadn't choked ..." He would have failed his second test in this mission. Arian would be dead and his failure would be complete. It shouldn't matter. He'd longed for the peace the death of his soul would bring, that's what he wanted after all. Why, then, did it suddenly feel like taking the easy way out?

Arian and Penny elbowed their way through the crowd towards the bar. The festivities were well underway with dancers gyrating to the music, couples pairing off in dark corners and sleazebags hanging out as close as possible to the beer on tap at the bar. Arian slapped away yet another faceless, groping hand. Where was her Greek hero now when she really needed rescuing?

"Two colas, thanks," she said to the bartender.

"No alcohol? You didn't like the ouzo?" he asked, taking a moment to smooth back his jet-black, smoothed-back hair.

"Damn near killed me." Her head still spun and she wondered how much of it her brain had absorbed through her nose. "Just plain cola, thanks."

He nodded and made a show of spritzing the liquid onto ice, adding a twist of lime and dropping a straw into each glass. "Four euros, please."

She handed over the cash and picked up a glass in each hand, then turned to find Penny. There she was on the dance floor, a flock of admirers watching her and clapping her on. Penny loved to dance. It was her way of ridding herself of her demons, she said. If only Arian could do the same without inhibition.

Wouldn't it be great to shake the apprehension, the feeling something really bad was about to happen? Gran had always said she was fey but Arian didn't believe in magic or psychic powers. She believed in science, facts and figures, and logical conclusions. Though that didn't explain why, when she was alone, the weight of unhappiness eased back onto her shoulders and the sense of not belonging grew stronger.

With a sigh, Arian turned back to the bar to look for a seat away from the beer on tap and the queue of tipsy males it attracted. Walking as quickly as she could while dodging wandering hands, she found a spot around the corner at the end of the bar. She placed her drinks on the counter and hopped up onto the barstool, turning her back on the dance floor action.

It reminded her far too much of the parties back home. Guys flirting with girls, all looking for a quickie before they moved on somewhere else. Not a single splash of romance in sight despite the venue name — Paradise. Was that what modern relationships were all about — casual sex, one night stands, friends with benefits? Surely not. There had to be more to life than finding the perfect bed partner, no strings attached.

As far as bed partners went, Craig sucked. The sex had never been great or fulfilling. It had always been about Craig's selfish satisfaction first. Then he'd found someone else. Someone who was happy to take what he gave, no strings attached. A coach's daughter, happy to be a WAG. They made the perfect for-now couple.

Scowling, she sipped at her coke. Better take it slow. She had no desire to fight her way through the crowd to find a loo.

"Looking a little lonely here in the corner. I'm off duty in about five minutes, until midnight." The bartender reached for her hand across the counter. "We could go someplace quiet."

The hairs on the back of her neck raised in warning. She pulled her hand out from under his. "Piss off, I'm not available."

He chuckled, a sound too forced to be humour. "That's what you say now. I bet I could change that. I like a girl with a bit of spirit." He leaned in to whisper against her cheek. "They're good in bed."

Arian's stomach rolled as she sensed the presence of evil. Maybe coming to Mykonos wasn't such a good idea after all. First the incident on the beach, now this … she couldn't explain the eeriness or sense of danger she felt in the air. "Which part of fuck off don't you understand?"

The bartender tightened slender fingers around her wrist, his grip like iron. "No need to be like that now, honey. My pad is warm and filled with wicked delights. You know you want a little … fun."

She pulled out of his hold. "You're messing with the wrong girl, buddy. I have to warn you —"

Chairs tumbled over like bowling pins, clanging to the floor as the man was yanked from behind the bar and over the counter. Arian swivelled on her seat to see Jax holding him in the air at arm's length as the bartender aimed a punch, and missed.

"The lady said no, arsehole." He let go, pushed hard and the man staggered back.

"Let him go," Odys bellowed above the music. He pulled Jax back and the man stumbled away. "You can deal with him later. We know what he's up to."

Jax nodded and flexed his shoulders. He turned to Arian. "You okay?"

Speechless, she nodded. Her eyes followed the hard lines of his body. Where had all that strength come from? Jax had held off the bartender with one hand, and hadn't even broken a sweat. He was all power and muscle but the bartender was no weakling either with his lean control. Arian placed a hand on his arm, feeling firm muscles flex beneath her fingers.

"Thank you. I'm okay." She withdrew her hand and rubbed at her wrist, not that it ached from the bartender's touch, but her palm sure as hell tingled from touching Jax. From the distant look in his eyes, he was far from impressed at having to rescue her twice in the space of a few minutes. She wondered what he'd be like if he smiled more, relaxed a little.

"May we?" Jax righted the tumbled chairs and placed them on either side of her.

Even as stand-offish as he was, he'd still be far better company than whiskey-breathing bartenders and beer-on-tap sleazebags. She shrugged. "Sure. That's twice in one night you've saved me, thank you."

"My pleasure."

Only it didn't sound like it was, she thought.

He raised a hand to attract the replacement bartender's attention. "Can I buy you a fresh drink?" Arian shook her head. "Two Greek Tigers, please," he said to the bartender.

"So," said Odys from her left, "where's your friend tonight?"

"She's somewhere on the dance floor." Arian stiffened her shoulders against the intensity rolling off Jax. Clearly he thought he was doing her a favour by sticking around. She hadn't asked for — and certainly didn't need — a reluctant bodyguard. "Maybe I should go and find her. I'm sure she'll be thirsty now." Arian made to move off the stool.

"Is that her drink?" Odys waved a hand to the still full glass where the ice had started to melt and raise the level of fluid. "You stay here. I'll find her and let her know where you are."

"Umm … okay, thanks." Arian smiled, thankful she didn't have to fight her way around the dance floor looking for Penny.

Protection for the night after her run in with the bartender from hell seemed like a good idea. Should she report his behaviour to management? No, why ruin a good holiday? No point making waves. Nothing had happened and she was safe now … if a little awkward in the presence of the man who'd come to her rescue yet again. She turned to Jax and stuck to friendly pub talk. "So, where are you from? You have a slight accent."

He frowned down at her. "Born in Greece and living in Oakleigh. I am Greek. You?"

His reluctance to talk confused her. Why bother sticking around if he didn't want to be there? "Fairfield. On holiday with your family? Your little girl is very cute."

Jax perched on the seat next to her. His arm brushed against hers, sending pleasant tingles along her nerve endings. She folded her arms on the bar counter.

"Ermioni is Helen's daughter. Odys, Helen and I go a long way back."

"Ah, childhood friends?"

Jax chuckled thoughtfully and the pleasant tingles spiked to race through her blood. "Something like that. What about you and your friend?" He rolled his shoulders and settled more comfortably on the chair.

Arian shrugged. Maybe she'd imagined his reluctance. "Penny and I were friends before we could walk. We're taking a break from reality."

If only he'd try to make it sound like he cared instead of coming across as making conversation while he waited for his friend to come back. Why did it feel like a stab to the heart? Arian sighed. What did it matter anyway? With the resort island so full of holidaymakers, it was unlikely they'd see each other again after tonight. Just as well, she didn't need this weird kind of attraction she felt for him because she was not in the market … for sex or anything else.

Penny bounced up to them with Odys in tow. "Wowser, it's bloody hot on that floor. Hey, Jax, nice to see you again. Odys here told me you got stalked by the guy who tried to kill you with the ouzo, Arian. That sucks. You okay?" She chugged a couple of mouthfuls of her coke and crunched on an ice cube.

Arian smiled. Penny's energy always left her out of breath. "Yeah, I'm good."

"Awesome, come on out and dance then. You guys coming?" She looked from Jax to Odys.

For a moment they hesitated, then shrugged. Jax held out his hand to help Arian off her seat. As she placed her hand in his, energy zapped between their palms. She looked up at him to find his blue gaze fixed on her face. He smiled reluctantly — a without-even-trying, heart-stopping, sizzling hot smile that dimpled his cheeks and shaped his very kissable lips. The crackle she'd felt between their palms travelled up to restart her heart before diving down to the place she swore she'd never allow another man near again — at least not for a long time anyway. She crossed her legs.

"Maybe I'll sit here for a while, hey? You guys go. I'll be fine."

"Then I will stay with you," said Jax, all traces of the beautiful smile gone and replaced by a scowl. "After the incident with the bartender earlier, I would not like you to be alone. There are others like him waiting for their chance to approach you." To prove his point, he looked towards a group of guys lounging against the wall, eyeing her and Penny off. "As drunk as they are, it could start a fight or you could find yourself in a compromising position no-one should be in. Please, *kyria*, allow us to be your guides tonight. We might not know each other well, but we have at least done each other a favour today."

Between the devil and the deep blue sea.

Better the devil you know. Jax raised an eyebrow at her.

She narrowed her eyes. He'd done it again. Read her mind. Now, he cocked his head to the side and held out his hand again. Arrogant perhaps, but he was right. She didn't like the look in their eyes, nor did she need any more trouble after today, so she placed her palm on his and let him help her down. He kept a hold on her hand until they reached the outer edges of the dance floor, where he turned and held her lightly at the waist.

She barely reached Jax's shoulder with her high heels on. He towered above her, all broad shoulders and firm chest. Unsure where to put her hands, she stiffened and fixed a stare at the unbuttoned vee of his shirt, her senses on high alert at the smell of his very sexy cologne so close to her nose.

With a sigh, he raised one of her hands to his shoulder and held the other firmly between their bodies. "At least try to look as if you're enjoying it?"

"I will if you will," she snapped. "I don't get why you're doing this if you don't want to?"

He stepped onto the floor and she followed. "Who says I don't want to?"

She treated him to her most scornful look, one that usually made men take a step back or, at the very least, stumble. Jax didn't even flinch. "Your body language is shouting so loudly the people across the room know you don't really want to dance with me."

His arm settled in the small of her back, securing her firmly against him. “Are you usually this easy to get along with?”

The sarcasm in his voice shouldn’t have hurt so much coming from a stranger but it did. Was he right? Was that why everyone she loved had left her — her mother, her brother and finally her father? Even her grandmother had gone. All she had left was Penny. Was that why she’d tried so damn hard to fit into Craig’s world and failed?

She blinked against the sting of tears and concentrated on following his dance steps instead. The man could dance, no doubt about it, and she wouldn’t expect less from a Greek. They were born with natural grace and rhythm. She shouldn’t feel so comfortable in his arms either now that she’d allowed herself to relax a little, especially not when reluctance warred with attraction.

And there was still that niggling doubt in her mind as to why he’d stood by, watching his friend’s little girl drown and not do anything. What man did that? What fear had held him frozen as the waves crashed around him? There’d been no hesitation in his rushing to her rescue tonight.

The crowded dance floor seemed to get smaller as he moved with her in his arms. Heat pooled in places it shouldn’t have. He was so damned sexy it was hard not to be drawn into his warmth, into the welcoming cradle of his hips … Not the best move, Arian thought, as their bodies brushed lightly against each other with each turn.

Two songs later, something between them shifted. What or how, she had no desire to question. She raised her eyes and met his burning gaze. Her doubt and restlessness faded in its wake. His eyes had darkened to the stormy blue you'd find far out to sea, and she felt the razor-sharpness sear her skin. With a little pressure on her back, he drew her closer and held her tighter as the music slowed. He folded her hand against his chest, letting her feel the rapid beat of his heart.

With a sigh, she let her head fall into the curve of his shoulder and closed her eyes. Safe. He felt solid and safe — like coming home — as if she belonged in his arms.

Damn it, what was he doing? Jax cursed himself for letting her get so close. He'd felt complete the moment he'd taken her in his arms and felt the sway of her body against his. The glass around his heart had shattered with the warmth of her hand pressed against it and she'd crept past the guard he would wear like armour around his soul if he had one.

She fit so well against him. His arms ached not to gather her too much closer, to keep some distance between them.

For a micro-second, Jax cupped her head in his hand and allowed his lips to whisper against her hair. The sweet-as-honey scent of her shampoo permeated his senses. Then his hand was at her waist again, guiding her gently around the dance floor until he felt the evening breeze at his back.

The cool night air did nothing to calm the feelings that churned inside him. He danced her out the door onto the terrace, his feet moving even though he wanted them to stop, until they reached the low wall overlooking the sea. Powerless except for emotions raging inside him he refused to give name to, he stood with his back against the concrete and held her against his chest.

One night, just one night of dancing … nothing else … and then he would watch her from afar and protect her only as ordered. He'd promised himself never to fall prey to a woman's wiles again, yet here he stood, unable to resist one more powerful than Athena and so far out of his league, he should not be anywhere except on his knees at her feet.

"We've stopped dancing," she murmured, snuggling closer against the cool breeze off the sea.

"Yes," he whispered, laying his head against hers.

It no longer mattered how long they stood that way, holding each other. It felt so right … as if he'd been there before. What magic was this? Had the potion Hades slipped in her drink made him feel this euphoria? He had drained all the poison from her system into his and neutralised it with his magic. Could it be some had stayed in his bloodstream to cause this infatuation?

But no, his head had been clear when he'd met with her at the bar, and what he felt now was nothing like the effects of a drug. The power to mess with his head was all Arian's.

At the back of his conscience, reason tried to weasel its way in. He should warn her against picking up men in nightclubs. The incident with Hades posing as a bartender was the perfect example of what happened when men hung out in clubs preying on women. He pushed the thought back. What could possibly be wrong with enjoying a little of the romance Paradise Beach offered just for one night?

He felt her shift against him and tuned in to her thoughts. They tumbled around in her mind, a mirror of his, except with a touch of insecurity and betrayal. Out here, with magic in the stars and the sound of the sea soothing his senses, he wanted to erase the turmoil that raged inside her.

"You think too much, little one. You carry so much pain inside you." At the feather-light touch of his forefinger on her chin, she opened her eyes and watched his lips descend on hers. All reasonable thought and doubt fled as he teased her mouth with a kiss, his tongue tracing the seam of her lips until they parted on a sigh. But instead of plundering and taking, Jax took his time testing and tasting until frustration danced with desire.

She crunched his shirt in her fists and pulled him closer. Jax adjusted his stance to fit her snugly between his legs and kissed her like she demanded to be kissed. Hot and hard, the way his body felt against hers. He pressed her against him, core to core and Arian reined in the overpowering need to brush against the hard length of him.

With one last taste of her lips, Jax raised his head a little and smiled. "Ah, Arian," he whispered. "You are like the nectar of the gods. The special brew Zeus keeps only for himself."

With a smile, Arian snuggled into him, enjoying the warmth of his body against hers. She snaked her arms around his waist and hugged him tightly, giving up trying to analyse the connection she felt to Jax. Somewhere between songs, he'd relaxed. Perhaps it was the music, or the dancing, perhaps it was the full moon or the enchantment of Paradise Beach. Whatever it was, she may as well make the best of it … who knew if or when she'd feel magic like this again?

He made no move to carry on where he'd left off. Instead, he seemed content to hold her, his hands gently stroking out a pattern on her back. What did he want from her? Was he just another sleazebag who pretended not to be interested, then took if it was offered anyway?

With each stroke of his hands at her back, her body tingled and yearned for more. He'd left his reluctance on the dance floor and now the connection between them had shifted from rigid tension to comfortable awareness.

Under her cheek, a soft laugh rumbled in his chest. "Just like Zeus' brew, it is a taste we need to enjoy slowly, to savour the full body and worship every drop."

How could she argue with that? Not when he made having sex sound like making love, and she didn't doubt for a moment that a night of passion was on the agenda. Maybe not tonight … maybe only in her dreams.

"This is no dream, my Faerie Queen," he said, placing a kiss on her head again.

Arian's eyes flew open and she stiffened against him. "How do you do that? How do you read my mind?"

His chest lifted and fell as he sighed. Gentle hands cupped her shoulders and steadied her back on her feet. "That is a story for another day, perhaps when I have earned your trust. Come, let's take a walk on the beach. If I stand here much longer with you in my arms, I am going to forget about going slow."

Her hand in his, they climbed down the steps of the terrace and onto the sandy beach. The gentle splash of the waves in the moonlight accompanied them as they walked. For the first time she could remember, she enjoyed the beauty of silence in any man's company. There were no awkward attempts at conversation, only the comfort of their entwined fingers and the warmth of his arm brushing hers as he guided her towards the old stone archway near the rocks.

Stepping under the arch, he sat down on the sand and drew her down beside him, placed an arm around her and tugged her close. "Comfortable?"

Arian nodded against his shoulder. "So, tell me about Jax Polemistis."

She looked up and studied his profile in the light of the moon. A soft, neatly trimmed beard brushed the strong curve of his jaw and caressed the bronzed skin under his cheekbones. Arian gathered enough courage to let her hand follow the curve of it to his ear, where she tucked away the length of his dark brown, wavy hair. It fell over the collar of his shirt, just long enough to be sexy as it curled at the nape. Her fingers retraced their steps to touch the curve of his bottom lip, a little fuller than the top one. He kissed her fingertips then drew her hand down to his chest where he anchored it against his heart.

"Not much to tell, really. I was born in Greece and have lived in Oakleigh for some years now. I'm a barrister by day and at night I wield a different sword of justice behind the bar at Odys' nightclub in Richmond."

Arian smiled. "You're a bouncer? You'd have to be fit and strong for that. Those blokes in Richmond can get a little feisty during footy season."

He chuckled and she thought she could grow used to the light laughter brought to his beautiful eyes. "Yes, I've had my share of black eyes over the years from the fights they start. What about you, Arianrhod, Queen of the Faeries?"

Arian smiled wistfully. "I'm no faerie, nor am I a queen. My gran used to call me her faerie princess though. She believed she was a mystical being, especially near the end. She had Alzheimer's but she could still tell a good tale. There was one she used to tell about a magical world called Paradise where once she was the queen. Gran would say I was her successor to the throne. I used to love her stories, even if they were far-fetched. I'll never be a queen or a princess, not even for Gran." Sadness at the memories threatened to close in but she shook it off. She missed Gran so much. "I'm just Arian Kendrick, a boring geographical surveyor born in St Kilda and raised in Fairfield."

"I cannot imagine there is anything boring about you, *agape mou.*"

"I bet you say that to all the girls you meet," Arian scoffed. Meaningless words he whispered knowing they'd never see each other again, but God help her he was hard to resist. Despite her doubts, some un-nameable, invisible cord wound around her heart and drew her closer. She traced her fingertips across the open collar of his shirt, brushing the smooth skin that lay beneath. Her finger dipped into the groove at the base of his strong neck and followed the path of his collarbone as far as the fabric of his shirt would allow.

Jax captured her wandering hand. "No, you will find I never say anything I don't mean." He tipped up her chin to look deep into her eyes. There was no mistaking the message in them. It burned through her, turning her insides to mush, touching the deepest, most secret, and right now, most sensitive spot in her body.

If a mere look could deliver an orgasm, she'd just experienced a multiple one. A shiver slipped through her and she leaned closer, drawn by the invisible cord that snapped and sparked between them. With a frustrated growl, Jax swept her onto his lap, crushed her against his chest and kissed her, long and hard, until her head spun and the wash of the waves faded away.

Of all the emotions that swept through her, fear was not one of them as he plundered her mouth, drinking his fill, draining her energy until she lay limp in his arms. His kiss became softer, less demanding as he stroked and soothed the goosebumps of desire from her skin. With infinite care now, he released her lips. Her eyes fluttered open to meet his.

"Wow ..."

Here was a man who knew how to kiss. If he wanted to claim her as his, he'd get no argument from her. He should come with a health warning — like a five-litre tub of full cream triple-choc ice-cream with nuts.

Her heart pounded in her chest and her breath came in short, sharp puffs. Gently he moved her off his lap and away from his obvious desire. She wasn't sure whether to feel rejected or relieved. Jax pushed himself up off the sand and held out a hand.

"Come, Arian," he said. "Let's walk back. This is not the place or the time." He pulled her up and into his arms, linking his hands at the curve of her spine. "When we make love, *agape mou*, it will be in comfort and private where I can show you endless hours of pleasure. Treasure you like you deserve to be treasured, and love you in a way that leaves no doubt fate meant us to meet."

Turning towards the club, they walked hand in hand, in silence. Arian, mind and body numb except for the tingle of desire in the region of her abdomen, realised that whoever Jax Polemistis was, he was no ordinary man because she swore her soul left Earth and she'd seen a slice of heaven when he'd kissed her.

It seemed like a good idea at the time. If ever there was a song written for him, it was that one. As he heard Arian slip the safety chain on her hotel room door into place, he rested his forehead against his fist on the corridor wall. His plan had backfired on him big time.

Bloody Hades. When he'd wrapped his hand around Arian's wrist, the intention was clear in the blackness of his aura. He'd had murder on his mind. If Ajax and Odys hadn't arrived in time, Arian would be gone. Her body would be found, but her soul would be trapped forever, wherever Hades decided to leave it. He knew who she was and he'd upped the stakes.

No way could he abandon Arian now. The warrior in him wouldn't allow it. The very thought of her lifeless, of her soul wandering in the mists for eternity, brought an ache to his heart he had no desire to explore. She's a woman, he reminded himself, a creature not to be trusted just like Athena. He'd practically fallen at her feet the moment his lips had touched hers. Whatever Hades had put in her drink, it was strong and now it flowed through his veins. What other explanation could there be for losing his common sense so completely over a woman again?

Had she flirted with Hades? Teased him and then carelessly rejected him? That would surely incite the devil's anger. It had certainly incited his in that field so long ago. And that's what women did best, wasn't it? They played with emotions and broke hearts, destroyed the power of clear thinking.

He'd studied their wiles for centuries. As women had thrown off the veil of suppression and embraced liberty, they'd grown bolder in their advances on men. No longer did they wait for a man to make the first move. No, instead they were the hunters and men their prey. Athena had taught women well, and bloody Cupid with his arrows had aided and abetted her in bringing mankind to their knees and at their mercy.

He refused to be one of the conquered. Sure, he'd enjoyed the company of a few women over time. He had needs to be met like any healthy adult male, but he'd made it clear he didn't want or need a relationship. If his heart wasn't involved he could maintain a clear head, and he'd been right to keep it that way. So why then did things feel different around Arian?

He drew away from the wall and shoved his fists into the pockets of his pants. When she'd relaxed against him on the dance floor, he'd thought it the perfect excuse. If he pretended a holiday romance with her, he could easily protect her while Zeus did his thing and got her to the throne. Then Zeus could explain to her how she really was the Faerie Queen, his job protecting her would be done and he could get on with his life — or death — whichever pleased Zeus the most. Easy … piece of cake and a jug of ambrosia. Except for one small problem … she'd bewitched him. Sucked him in, kissed him back and stolen a piece of his heart.

Never trust a damn faerie, whether they knew they were one or not. Athena had drawn him in the same way with beauty and charm that disguised a cold heart and a mean streak. Yet his gut told him Arian was different, and since his head had failed him so often in the past, all he had to go on now was instinct.

He'd felt her pain echoed in his heart, her emptiness, her loneliness as if it were his own. God help him, they were both tortured souls. Neither of them belonged where they were placed, nor did they deserve this eternal purgatory they found themselves in. The only difference between them was that he had already lost everything to fight for. Arian's battle was still to come.

CHAPTER THREE

"You saw stars?" Penny slapped sunscreen onto her legs with energy she shouldn't have after a night of dancing.

"I saw heaven," Arian corrected.

"Wow, must have been some kiss."

Arian sighed and lay back on the sun lounge. "Bloody oath it was."

"Or damn good drugs." Penny apparently couldn't let go of her drink-spiking theory. "And he didn't try to talk you into going back to his hotel room?"

"No. He walked me to the door, kissed me on both cheeks and told me he'd find me today." She sighed again. "He said it like he meant it."

"I guess he did. Here they come now." Penny waved the bottle of lotion to her left.

Arian watched as the small group headed their way. Jax and Odys swung little Ermioni between them, laughing at her giggles. Helen, wearing a colourful sarong, sang a little ditty that sounded like a nursery rhyme, but not one Arian recognised.

Her gaze wandered to Jax. Shirtless, his bronzed body gleamed with sunscreen, all wide shoulders, defined collarbones, and muscles with a healthy bulge. Not steroid enhanced muscles. These were honed to perfection. She admired his pecs, felt the urge to trace them with her hands all the way down to his six-pack and beyond the waistband of those damn fine bathers.

"Ladies," said Odys, stopping in front of them. "Mind if we join you?"

"Sure," said Penny and made space for his bulk at the bottom of her lounger.

Odys laughed so hard, Arian thought the sand moved. "Oh, honey, if I sit down there, you'll be catapulted into the sea. Put those lovely legs back. I'll sit here on the sand."

She watched with amusement as Penny eyed out Odys, caught his cocky look and blushed as she eased her legs back. Arian pondered for a moment on the fact Penny had actually blushed. The girl who Googled men's body bits, who could discuss the pros and cons of fellatio without so much as flush, had cheeks pinker than a peach, and it had nothing to do with the sun. There was something to tease Penny about later.

Arian turned her head as Jax knelt next to her in the sand. "Sleep well?" His eyes held hers.

No. I dreamt of you and woke up frustrated. "Yes, fine thanks."

I dreamt of you too. "That's good." He smiled.

"I see Ermioni has recovered from her battle with the wave yesterday." Arian smiled at Helen and tried not to shiver at the memory of the thing she'd faced down there or how close the little girl had come to drowning.

Helen studied Arian for a long moment — like a precious metal under a microscope — weighing, surveying and searching for clues as to the elements it consisted of. Whatever the ingredient it was she looked for, she must have found it because she smiled and nodded.

"Yes, thankfully she has made a remarkable recovery. I cannot thank you enough for going in after her. It was a very brave and selfless thing you did."

"To see her out here today, alive and happy, is all the thanks I need." Arian turned her attention to the little girl who stood looking at her with big brown eyes. "Hello." Ermioni gave a little wave and attached herself to Jax's side. Arian reached out to ruffle her curly head. Ermioni giggled and nudged her hand away. "You're a sweetie pie."

"Sweetie pie," repeated Ermioni and scrambled up onto the lounger next to her. "Dolly." She pulled a battered plastic doll from the pocket of her towelling beach robe and thrust it at Arian.

"Pretty," said Arian, smoothing down the synthetic blonde hair, hacked in zigzags on one side and crinkled from too many dips in the ocean.

"You pretty." The little girl wrapped the end of Arian's ponytail around her little fingers.

"Thank you, Ermioni. You're pretty too." She turned to look at Jax and found him staring at her with an odd yearning in his eyes. "What?"

A smile broke through his frown. "Nothing, nothing at all. I'm glad you like children. Ermioni's a pretty cool kid, aren't you, precious?" He tickled her ribs and Ermioni giggled. "Did you girls have plans for today? We're taking the boat out to a cove a few kilometres from here. Want to come along?"

"Sure, that would be nice," Penny answered.

Arian lifted her focus from Jax's smile and met his gaze. Tingles of awareness, and something very close to lust, danced through her senses as her imagination gave her a glimpse of twisted sheets, the slow movement of two bodies and sighs of pleasure. She blushed. "Okay," she choked out.

"Great, we'll meet you down at the pier in half an hour." Odys stood and dusted the sand from his shorts.

"See you later," said Jax, his gaze making goosebumps rise on her skin as her eyelashes fluttered down and the heat of a blush swept her cheeks.

"Yes," she whispered back, ignoring Penny's mocking snort.

As Jax rose and walked down the beach, stopping once to glance over his shoulder, Penny shook her head and said, "You've got it bad, sister, but not as bad as he does."

"A holiday affair, that's all it will be if it's anything at all," insisted Arian.

"Hah, we'll see about that," replied Penny, swinging her legs off the sun lounge.

"Is that right? Well whose cheeks are a pretty pink right about now?"

Penny swatted her with the soft material of her sun hat and changed the subject. "What kinda boat do you reckon they've got?"

Half an hour later, the forty-eight foot cruiser sailed the gentle seas with a style and elegance Arian envied. At the wheel, Penny nagged Odys to let her steer and she smiled at the banter between the two. She wondered if the spark between Odys and Penny was as strong as hers and Jax's, and if they even realised they made the perfect couple. Penny with her sunshine blonde hair, endless energy and wit. Odys with his easy humour and good nature.

She turned her attention to Helen and Ermioni. A spark of jealousy touched her heart as Jax leaned over to kiss Helen's cheeks. Was there something between them? Where was Ermioni's father? Tension crept up her spine. What if Jax … No, no speculation and it wasn't any of her business anyway. As if sensing her eyes on him, Jax looked up and waved. She waved back and turned her attention to the ocean instead. Crystal clear blue water surrounded them, the coastline a small speck on the horizon. She watched fish swim alongside the boat, chasing the wake.

"More wine?" Jax held a bottle of Sauvignon Blanc in one hand — so cold the condensation dripped from the glass — and a bucket of ice in the other.

"Thanks." She held up her glass while he poured.

He placed the bucket on the floor, capped the bottle and dropped it into the bucket. "Cheers," he said, touching his glass to hers.

"Cheers. This is beautiful, Jax. Thank you for inviting us along."

"So polite now, Arian. So distant all of a sudden. Why?" He covered her hand with his. When she opened her mouth to speak, he said, "And please don't tell me it's nothing."

She looked down as he entwined his fingers with hers. "You and Helen, have you ever ...?"

"Been lovers? No. Helen was married, but she is divorced now. To me, she is more like a sister."

"She's a beautiful girl. It must be hard raising a little one alone."

Jax squeezed her fingers. "Helen is a very strong woman and one to be admired. That is all we will ever be, good friends."

"Your bond is strong." Arian tamped down the jealousy that swelled in her heart. Helen was a lucky woman to earn that respect. Perhaps one day, she too could have that special bond with someone. Just not today.

Jax paused for a long moment until Arian thought he might not respond. She didn't want to explore what his hesitation might mean.

"Stronger than most would understand."

"Oh." Arian frowned.

"It's a very long story. Not one I think you want to hear today. All I ask is that you believe me when I tell you there is nothing but friendship between us. Let's enjoy the sunshine now."

Arian agreed and sipped at her wine, but the thoughts churned in her head. Last night he'd avoided talking about himself and now he avoided talking about his relationship with Helen, yet he wanted her to trust him? How many times had Craig said the same thing? *Trust me, Arian, there's nothing going on between me and the coach's daughter. Why would I cheat on you? Why would I lie to you?* Yet he had, more than once. If she couldn't trust a man she knew well, how could she trust one she didn't?

At least Craig's cheating ways were no longer her problem, even though the trust issues remained. Her only regret was not leaving the bastard sooner, that she'd put up with his spoilt superstar behaviour and the lousy sex for as long as she had. And why the hell was she even thinking of that dirty stinking spineless rat on a beautiful day like today out on the Aegean Sea, living the dream with a man-god at her side?

Jax sat close, his thigh touching hers, his arm across the back of the padded seat behind her shoulders. She pushed aside her doubts to answer his questions about aerial photography and her degree in surveying — much safer ground. She asked about his job as a barrister, the club Odys owned back in Melbourne and what he liked to do for fun — everything except the mystery that shrouded Helen.

"Jax, can I ask you something?" she said, as a comfortable lull fell on their conversation.

"Of course, *agape mou*, anything you like."

"What happened yesterday?" She felt him stiffen beside her, the knuckles on his hand around the wine glass turning white as he clenched it harder.

"What do you mean?"

"You ..."

Oh God, why had she started this? Why was it so damn important to her that he have a bloody good reason for not diving in head first into the sea to save Ermioni? Unlike her father, who'd been a champion swimmer and lifeguard with all the skills he'd needed to save Timmy's life, and hadn't been able to.

"You didn't go in after Ermioni. Why?" There she'd said it, and the moment the words were out of her mouth, she regretted them.

He pulled his arm from around her and stood. Tossing the contents of his glass over the side of the boat, he picked up the empty bottle from the deck. "I lost my nerve. That's the only excuse I have. A lousy one, *nai?* If you weren't there … I am a coward."

He shook his head, his back stiff and his shoulders pulled back. Arian felt the walls slam up around him and lock her out. "Jax, it's okay. I shouldn't have asked ..."

"No, you have every right to question me, Arian. I am not the man you think I am." Odys shouted down from the helm for Jax to get ready to anchor. He turned away from her, but not before she saw the pain in his eyes and regretted putting it there. "Ready for a swim to shore?"

In the flurry of activity that followed, Arian pushed the moment and the mystery that surrounded the group of friends to the back of her mind. Helen and Ermioni rowed to shore in the little inflatable dinghy with the picnic basket and cooler filled with drinks while the rest of the group opted to swim. It turned into a contest between Odys and Jax as they thrashed out and powered through the water.

Boys would be boys no matter what age they were, everything was a competition, with or without a prize. It was all about one-upmanship and ego. That's why they played sport — because they always had to win the battle. Isn't that what made them warriors? Or in Craig's case, arseholes.

Arian's edginess grew with each stroke and kick of powerful arms and legs in their testosterone display. "Penny, there's something very strange going on here."

"Like what?"

"I don't know. I can't put my finger on it. Some things just aren't adding up. First up, how the hell can they swim so fast?" She pointed to where Odys rose from the water a hair's breadth ahead of Jax.

"Superhuman men of muscle?" Penny teased. "Maybe they trained for the Rottnest Challenge or to outswim the crocs in the Northern Territory for sport."

"I'm serious." She splashed water at Penny with a scoop of her hand. "The mind reading … seeing heaven in a kiss … the whole zapping thing?"

"I still think your ouzo was spiked. The bartender looked a little odd, a little devilish really, with that jet-black hair, black eyes and goatee."

"Oi, what's taking you girls so long?" Odys called across the water.

"Coming." To Arian she said, "Hey, look. After this, we may never see them again. Does it matter that they have secrets? Do you like Jax?"

There was no need for hesitation. "Yes."

"Then go for it, girlfriend. Don't miss out on an opportunity because you like to overthink things." With that sage advice, she struck out at her best competitive pace.

Arian sighed and followed. Perhaps Penny was right and she was thinking too much.

Jax watched the expressions flit across Arian's face as they sat nibbling at the delights of the picnic basket. Whether he liked it or not, the easiest way to keep an eye on Arian was to play the role of an attentive admirer. As long as he could keep it light-hearted and at fling level, it would be fine. As long as he remembered it wasn't real and kept up his levels of mistrust around her, he wouldn't fall hard for her soft laugh and ethereal qualities.

So why was he so damned tuned in to her aura? And why had it felt like a sword through his heart when she'd questioned his actions on the beach? He could have told her the truth, but he doubted she'd believe him. He'd yet to convince her she was a queen. That would be hard enough. This whole task was spiralling out of control and he didn't like it one bit.

He'd felt her retreat as she studied the group carefully when she thought no-one was looking. It was tempting to take a peek at her thoughts, to listen to what was going on behind those beautiful green eyes. He resisted, fairly sure he wouldn't like what he'd hear.

"More wine," he asked, touching her hand.

She shook her head. "Any more and I'll go to sleep. It's lovely here, Jax, the warm sun, the calm water, the company."

He wrapped his fingers around hers and tugged her closer. Damned if it didn't feel good having her there at his side. Maybe just for this one day, he could let his guard down a little and enjoy life. He hadn't had a lot of fun in two thousand years, give or take. All he needed to do when they got back to Paradise Beach was remember to put the guard around his heart back in place.

Lulled by the wine and peacefulness of the cove, Arian let her head rest on his shoulder, enjoying the warmth of his skin under her cheek. She inhaled the smell of him, a mixture of coconut-scented sunscreen and man. It would be so easy to take what he offered, but what about after, when the Greek sunshine gave way to the changing moods of Melbourne's weather? Would he still want her then? Would she still want him?

"Okay, c'mon, guys, I want to know more about you." Penny's voice interrupted her thoughts. "What's with your names? All the Greek guys I know back in Melbourne have names like Tom and Andrew."

Odys laughed, a deep belly laugh that echoed around the cove. "And you know so many, Penny?"

Penny picked a grape off the bunch he held in his hand. "Hundreds, yes. So, Odys, tell me."

If Arian hadn't turned her attention to Odys when he'd laughed, she would have missed the enquiring look he sent Jax. She shivered against him and felt his arm tighten around her. It did nothing to abate the nerves that whirled in her stomach. There were definitely secrets kept in this tight-knit group.

"Our parents were a little … old-fashioned … I guess would be the right word. They chose ancient Greek names for their sons. Legend has it we're descendants of the gods for whom we're named."

Penny snorted her disbelief. "Sure you are."

"It's true. Now listen up," he continued. "My name is Odysseus Laertiades. I am the descendant of Laertes, King of the Cephallenians."

"A prince? Now that's a fairytale if ever there was one." Penny laughed.

Odys reached out and ruffled her hair. "Do you want to know the story or not?"

She sighed. "Yes, of course I do."

"Then be quiet a moment, *kopelis*. Now, Laertes is the

son of Arcesius, who is rumoured to be the son of Zeus. Things got a little messy in Greek mythology at times."

"My head is spinning already. So Odys is a descendant of Zeus. That's as much as I can handle right now," Penny wrapped it up neatly, although Arian could tell she was enthralled by the story. "Your turn, Jax."

"Haven't you had enough mythology for one day, Penny?" Jax groaned.

She snagged another grape from Odys' bunch, wiggling closer. "It's fascinating. We didn't come to Greece just for the view. Spectacular as it is ..."

"Why don't we have another drink instead?" suggested Jax.

Arian sat up. "Come on, Jax. I'd like to know too."

Jax sighed, took his arm from around Arian's shoulders and refilled their wine glasses. He settled back against a rock and stretched his long legs out in front of him. Little Ermioni crawled onto his lap and snuggled against the warmth of his chest, her eyelids drooping.

A pang of jealousy crept into her heart. Ridiculous … how could she be jealous of such a sweet little girl? Ermioni popped her thumb in her mouth and settled down against Jax to sleep. With a gentle hand, he stroked her curls. He'd make a perfect father, Arian thought.

"I am Ajax Polemistis —" He broke off as Penny giggled. "What?"

"Your mother named you after a detergent?"

Jax laughed. "Don't be cheeky, Miss Penny. Zeus is pretty accurate at aiming his lightning bolts."

Arian looked up at the clear blue sky and hoped he was wrong. She didn't want anything to spoil the day. "Ajax?" she prompted.

He grinned. "I am related to Ajax the Great, son of Aeacus who is the grandson of Zeus, and cousin to Achilles."

"Achilles, the greatest warrior of all time, hero of the Trojan War?" Penny's interest sparked, her eyes wide.

"Yep, that's the one. Ajax and Odysseus became the heroes who fought the Trojans to get Achilles' body back for burial when he was killed in battle. Ajax drove off the Trojans with his great shield and spear while Odysseus loaded the body into his chariot, and rode away to safety."

Enthralled by the story and the pure magic of his voice, Arian moved to sit next to Jax. He welcomed her with that sexy smile and cuddled her close, one arm around her, the other supporting a sleeping Ermioni. With a kiss on Arian's temple, he continued.

"Achilles had a shield of magic forged for him on Mount Olympus by the god Hephaestus. After the burial, the Greek leaders decided to award the Shield of Achilles to the warrior who most deserved it. After days of debate over who had earned it more, Odysseus and Ajax tied for ownership of the magical armour. Ajax argued that he deserved the shield because of his strength and commitment in war to the Greeks, including saving their ships from destruction. Good old Odysseus though — the smooth talker he is — persuaded the council to give him the armour."

"Greedy bugger." Penny shot Odys a look.

"Hey!" He retaliated by tugging her long blonde ponytail. "Who wouldn't want magic armour? Those spears the enemy wielded were bloody sharp, I tell you. Rip a hole right through you and push your insides out the other side."

"Gross," squealed Penny.

"Ignore her, Jax, carry on."

"Penny's right. It gets pretty gruesome after that."

"It's Greek mythology. I'd expect nothing less than all the gory details," said Penny.

"The truth gets a little twisted here and the argument has left Greeks divided for centuries. Some say he committed suicide because he was ashamed at his loss to the lesser man, Odysseus."

"Say what?" Odys boomed. "Who are you calling a lesser man?"

"Shh, you'll wake Ermioni." Helen, who until that moment had remained silent, slapped Odys on the foot with a tea towel. "Behave and let Jax finish."

Jax grinned. "Anyway, after the armour was awarded to Odysseus, Ajax was furious. He'd fought so hard to hold back the Trojans so Achilles could have the hero's funeral he deserved, rather than be left to the vultures on the battlefield."

His eyes darkened with sadness and Arian wondered why he felt the pain of his ancestor so deeply. She watched his throat work as he paused for a moment, felt his body stiffen against hers.

"Drowning his loss in ambrosia, he decided to kill Odysseus and the Achaean leaders. That way the Shield of Achilles would be his. Greed made him ugly and jealousy made him angry. Athena visited him in the field that night. She tempted him with her body and cast a spell on his mind. He fell asleep and awoke delusional. Hallucinations made him think a flock of sheep were the Achaean leaders, and the ram he slaughtered was Odysseus. Later, when he came to his senses covered in blood, surrounded by dead sheep, he realised he'd diminished his honour and killed himself rather than live with the shame."

"Oh my God, why would Athena do that to him?" Arian sat up and placed a hand on his arm, the horror of Ajax's story far too vivid in her mind. His skin was cool beneath her palm as he answered.

"Athena was in love with Odysseus. She was his protector. She'd rather see Ajax dead than Odysseus murdered, so she diminished his honour in the worst possible way. She drove him insane, knowing that if the Greeks didn't have him killed for what he intended to do, the gods would. Ajax had lost what he wanted most in life, the shield. Mortified by his actions, and that he'd plotted to kill his best friend, he decided there was nothing left for him to live for anyway."

"There's more to life than wealth and possessions, a lesson Ajax failed to learn," Odys said, looking squarely at Jax.

"Like betrayal, war and hate?"

"No … like love, trust and friendship. Not everyone is like Athena, Jax. The Greeks would have understood if it was explained to them. Your … Ajax's brother wanted to leave *his* body in that field for the vultures to pick at but it was Odysseus, the man he'd wanted to murder, who arranged for the respected warrior to have the burial he deserved. His death should never have happened. If Odysseus had had more patience that day and seen it for the ruse it was, he could have prevented Ajax's suicide. Instead he was blinded by his own anger and greed, and couldn't see the pain his friend was in."

Arian looked from one man to the other. *What the hell?* Anger flared in Odys's eyes and Jax narrowed his. Judging by the way their bodies tensed, the story had become almost … personal. The disquiet that had settled in the pit of Arian's stomach during Jax's storytelling resurfaced. The sands shifted beneath them and the sky above darkened with storm clouds.

Helen interrupted the moment with a low growl. "Boys, that's enough. Come, Jax, finish the story. We should make our way back to shore soon. It's getting late and there's a storm coming."

Jax relaxed a little. "He fell on his sword, preferring death to dishonour, that's it."

"Coward's way out," said Odys.

"Fuck you, Odys."

Odys stood, brushed the sand from his bathers and shrugged. "So you tell me every time we revisit that story. There was an alternative."

"What? Did you think Zeus would believe Athena was a manipulative little bitch?" Anger and bitterness coloured Jax's tone, turning his sensuous lips into a sneer Arian wasn't sure she liked.

Penny looked at Arian, her eyebrows raised. Arian sent her a silent message back. *What is going on?*

"I think he knew that well enough. Why do you think he —?"

Helen stood and placed a firm hand on Odys' chest. "Time to go. Start packing up."

For a moment, Arian thought he was going to move Helen aside and advance on Jax. He hesitated, obviously thinking better of it, and nodded. "Yes, before the tide changes."

As he turned to pack up, Helen reached down to pick Ermioni up from Jax's lap. "I'll settle her in the dinghy while you clear the picnic away." She turned her attention to Arian and Penny. "Please excuse us a moment? I need a little chat with these boys. Would you girls mind swimming back to the boat and waiting there for us? It won't take long."

Arian stood and looked uncertainly at Jax. He nodded. "It's okay, Arian. Go ahead. Put the coffee machine on in the galley below deck and we'll have something warm before we head back."

Without a word, Penny and Arian headed for the water, happy to escape the sudden tension between the three.

"Well, that was awkward," said Penny, towelling the sea water from her legs. "Either they take their Greek mythology very seriously or there was some subliminal message in that story."

Arian shook her hair free from the rubber band and brushed the dark red length. She wound it in a coil and squeezed out the excess water. The vibes between the three bounced across the water and she wasn't sure she liked the tone of them. Keeping secrets was one thing, but the retelling of a myth shouldn't evoke such anger.

Looking back at the three people on the beach, she replied, "I think we're in too deep here, Penny. Maybe we shouldn't see them again."

"Come on, Arian. It was a little dispute over something we don't understand. It's obvious they know each other well enough to share secrets. I doubt they're going to turn into axe murderers or people traffickers."

"I know, but right now there are too many questions in my mind. There's something … I don't know … odd that I can't quite put my finger on. When Jax and Odys were arguing, did you feel the sand shifting?"

"Well, yeah … no … kinda." Penny shrugged. "I thought I'd had too much sun and wine. Helen did say there was a storm brewing. Perhaps it's that."

"Maybe it was a coincidence. We're surrounded by volcanic matter. It might have been a little rumble, I suppose. It was just kinda weird, that's all."

"Hold that thought and go put the coffee machine on. Helen's getting into the dinghy."

Arian made her way to the cabin and located the coffee machine in the tiny galley. Her thoughts ticked over at a million miles an hour as she replayed the conversation in her head. Helen, Odysseus and Ajax — she tried to remember her myths. If she believed in magic and fairy tales like her gran had, she might believe they *were* legends reincarnated but she didn't, so it had to be the wine that made her feel like Jax and Odys had actually been at the Battle of Troy during the telling of that story.

She sighed. Just her luck. Finally she'd found a man who was sexy, kind and caring, and he turned out to be some kind of telepathic loony who believed he was a god.

In his defence, he kissed like one and looked like one with all that golden muscle, the sexy beard and wavy hair. And, oh that smile. One hot package but was it worth risking her sanity for a holiday bonk? No, there'd be nothing simple about sex with Jax. If she saw heaven in his kiss, what would she see if they took it to the bedroom?

She heard Penny call out to Helen and looked up the stairs towards the backboard. Penny secured the line and pulled the dinghy closer. Arian climbed out of the cabin to help unload.

"Can you take Ermioni for me?"

Arian smiled down at her. "Of course, pass her up."

She held out her arms for the little girl. Helen placed the sleeping child into Arian's arms. Immediately Ermioni snuggled against her and Arian felt her heart contract. For a moment, she took in the sweet little face, flushed with sleep and sun, the Cupid's bow lips pursed and moist with lip balm. Ermioni's mop of curly dark hair felt like silk against her skin. A little doll. She tightened her arms around her protectively. A vision of two little girls and a boy, all similar to Ermioni, flashed through her mind. The little boy looked exactly like Jax.

Arian drew in a breath and chased the picture from her mind. She took a step towards the cabin and stopped at Helen's voice.

"Girls, I'm so sorry about what happened back there. Those two can get carried away. Every time they tell it, it becomes a competition, a challenge they both have to win."

Arian and Penny murmured in unison, "That's okay."

"I've given them ten minutes to sort themselves out." She smiled. "Don't be surprised if one of them comes back with a black eye or a split lip. Bloody men and their testosterone."

Arian smiled back. "I've put the coffee machine on. I'll put Ermioni down in the cabin, shall I?"

"Yes, thank you … and, Arian?" Arian turned back. "Jax really likes you. Please don't be put off by this … weirdness. There are simply things he cannot explain to you right now. He will when the time is right."

Great, more weirdness, thought Arian. "Right. Okay then." She seriously considered the soundness of her own mind as the men returned to the boat and they set sail for Paradise Beach.

An hour later they sailed into the small harbour. Helen was right, Arian thought. Odys had a split lip and Jax sported a bruised cheek. As Arian and Penny gathered their things, Odys prepared to help them onto the jetty where Jax waited to give them a hand across the gap.

"There we go, ladies. I'm sorry our little … disagreement … got in the way of an otherwise pleasant day."

"No worries," said Penny. "Thank you for taking us out. We enjoyed the cove."

"Yes," Arian agreed quickly. "We had a lovely time."

Odys smiled. "Who's first?"

Penny put her hand up and Odys helped her across to Jax. Placing his hands on Arian's shoulders, he said quietly, "I'm really sorry, Arian. I spoilt it for you. Jax has a bad habit of giving up too easily on an argument sometimes. I needed to remind him that some things are worth fighting for, and not always the ones you think are worth winning."

"It's none of my business, Odys." Arian bit back the apprehension that churned in her stomach.

"Not yet but it will be soon," replied Odys. On that cryptic note, he turned her around and thrust her across to where Jax waited, arms outstretched and a fierce look on his face.

Jax held her against him for a long moment, his strong arms firm against her back, her breasts flattened against the expanse of his chest. His heart thudded against hers as he looked deep into her eyes.

"I'm sorry if our argument scared you back there. We're a family and like brothers, our discussions often become heated. There are things I should explain … perhaps later?"

"There's no need," Arian said.

He rested his forehead against hers for a brief moment before kissing the tip of her nose. "There is every need for you to understand. I'll see you a little later up at the hotel?"

"Umm … maybe we should … I think Penny and I ..." Arian looked at Penny for help. Perhaps it was best they put some distance between themselves and the complexity of the relationship between these three.

Jax nodded and let Arian slip down the length of his body until her feet touched the jetty. "Yes, I understand." His arms slipped from around her.

The shame in his eyes tore at her heart, but she needed space to think, to ponder on the day's events and the outcome. Complications, secrets and lies no longer had a place in her life. She'd left all that behind with Craig.

"Thank you for a lovely day, for everything." Arian stepped away from him and picked up her beach bag. She cursed the doubts that clouded her mind and the secrets the small group kept between them because, in that moment, her heart ached just a little for whatever it was that put the pain in his eyes. "We'll see you around."

Jax nodded sadly, his eyes on the horizon beyond her head. With one last look, Arian turned away from the man she thought might be the right one for her.

Arian and Penny walked along the jetty to the beach in

silence. Once out of range of hearing of the others, Penny said, "Jeez Louise, you okay, hon?" She heaved a sigh of relief.

Arian nodded, not sure she could speak past the massive lump in her throat. Tears of disappointment pricked at her eyelids. She dropped her sunglasses from her head onto her nose to hide them as little drops trickled out the corners of her eyes.

"Finding Mr Right sucks," she muttered and swiped at her cheeks. "Just when you think you've found him, it all turns weird on you."

"I'm sure there's a perfectly sane explanation for this." Penny paused for the automatic door to the hotel foyer to slide open. "While you pour us a glass of wine, I'm going to Google me some Greek mythology."

Arian hiccupped on a laugh. "You think you'll find the answers?"

"No," said Penny, linking an arm through hers, "but it's going to be bloody entertaining finding out why Athena was such a little bitch."

"And what exactly went on between Ajax and Odysseus, although I'm not sure about the part where he falls on his sword." Arian shivered. "Sounds a little gruesome."

"Bloody oath, I hope there are pictures." Penny grinned.

Arian shook her head. That's why she loved Penny. No matter what the drama or disaster, Penny was always there to lighten it up. Now if she could just get rid of the rock that weighed her heart down in her chest and picture a future without a certain god of Oakleigh, she'd be alright.

CHAPTER FOUR

"*Ilíthios. Anóitos.* What the hell were you thinking back there?" Helen's eyes flashed with anger as she stood in front of Jax and Odys. "Jax, you have to rein in that bloody temper of yours. If I hadn't stopped the two of you when I did, you would have started a goddamn earthquake. Did you two not feel the sand shifting under you?" She looked from one to the other. "No, of course not. You were too busy having a pissing competition."

"Helen—"

"Be quiet, Odys. I'm not done. What do you think those two girls would have thought if Zeus decided to send a lightning bolt out of a clear blue sky to knock you both on your arses? They're scared enough as it is now. They don't need a category five cyclone to chase them off any further."

"Helen —"

"Not your turn yet either, Ajax. There's no point finding the one you're meant to protect and then scaring her off with your goddam chest bumping. Did the two of you not understand Zeus' instructions at all?" She stamped her foot, rocking the boat with the force of it. Thunder growled in the sky. "Find the Faerie Queen and keep her safe. Not have another stupid fight that ends up with one of you either falling on your sword or being struck down for disobeying the one who gave you your lives back." Her body shook with anger now and energy zapped around her.

"*Helen,*" yelled Jax and Odys together.

"Stop," said Jax, pointing to the darkening sky.

Helen looked up. "Oh shit. See now? See what you made me do?" She closed her eyes and breathed in deeply through her mouth and out through her nose, holding her hands out, palms up. The energy around her fizzled and popped like wet fireworks as the gathering storm clouds cleared.

While Helen calmed the storm she'd started, Jax turned to Odys. "Did you mean what you said when you called me a coward?"

Odys shrugged. "There is nothing cowardly about holding off an army of thousands single-handedly to recover a mate's body from the battlefield. That's the stuff true chieftains are made of, courage far greater than anything I am capable of. You could have died that day, sacrificed yourself so I could transport Achilles' body away safely. Nor is it weak to have fallen prey to Athena's spell."

"So you believe me then?"

"I always have, Jax. It's Zeus you have to convince that you're worthy of a second chance at life and happiness. The only reason I fought for the Shield of

Achilles was because I wanted you to fight harder for it. For you to prove to Zeus you'd earned it."

"Well, since you put it that way ..." Jax aimed a smug smile at Odys.

"Dickhead, why do I have to remind you who of us is the more experienced chieftain? One day that damned ego of yours is going to be bigger than your head. Sky's clearing." He pointed up. "You done with us, Helen? I need a drink."

"For now … Jax, you've got some kissing up to do. I damn well hope nothing's happened to Arian while you two have been behaving like schoolboys. I spotted Hades hanging around the hotel pool before we left. Odys, do you think you can keep Penny out of the way for a while?"

It was Odys' turn for a smug smile. "Try and stop me. She's quite a package. A little verbal sparring with that dynamo is exactly what I need."

Helen shook her head. "Make sure you apologise for your bad behaviour first. Right, let's clean up and get out of here. Ermioni and I need a little peace and quiet on our own. And I'll need to explain the bloody storm to Zeus so he can reconfigure the weather satellite transmissions. I'll be filling out damned paperwork until Ermioni turns twenty-one, babysitting the two of you."

Arian sat on the balcony of their hotel room, nursing a glass of wine and watching the dark storm clouds over the harbour evaporate. She made a mental note to check for recent seismic activity in the area. Shifting sands in the cove earlier, freak storm clouds and a sudden swell around where the boats were docked — too many coincidences to rule out renewed volcanic activity in the area.

Anything to distract her from thinking about Jax. She tuned out Penny's voice reading aloud the information she'd dug up on the internet. It was too far-fetched to believe Jax and Odys were real gods anyway, so what did the age-old myth matter?

She rested her head against the back of the chair and allowed her eyes to drift closed. In her mind, she pictured Jax as she'd seen him on the trip home. He'd stared off into nothingness, his dark eyes troubled and jaw tensed. Silence had stretched between them, uncomfortable for the first time since they'd met. Her heart ached a little at the distance she'd chosen to put between them, but trust went hand in hand with attraction and right now, Jax had a question mark against the trust factor.

The hotel door shook as someone hammered on it. Penny jumped and squealed.

"Holy shit, don't break the door down, I'm coming." She put her laptop on the floor and made to get out of the chair.

Arian put a hand on her arm. "You stay. I'll get it. It's probably room service bringing back the dry cleaning."

"Right, I'll keep reading then." Penny grinned.

Arian stood and walked to the door. She pulled it open, hand out, ready to accept their clothes back. Instead she looked straight at Jax's chest. Her heart did a little pitter patter and stuck in her throat.

He leaned with his shoulder against the doorframe, arms folded, ankles crossed, looking every bit the part of a god come down from Olympus. She let her gaze travel over him, from the leather deck shoes, up the navy cargo shorts, over the white and blue striped shirt, until she met the intensity of his dark eyes.

"Hey," he said quietly.

"Hey." Her grip tightened on the door handle.

"I wanted to apologise again." His warm hand cupped her cheek, stroking the skin with his thumb. "I'm truly sorry."

Each stroke sent little shocks through her nerve endings, stirred her blood and robbed her of breath.

"Who is it, Arian?" called Penny.

Arian had trouble finding her voice. Jax smiled down at her and answered instead. "It's me, Penny. Odys wants to buy you a drink in the bar to apologise," he said, not taking his eyes off Arian.

"All of us?"

"We'll be down later. I have something to say to Arian first."

"Righto, I'll get my shoes," Penny called back. "I hope he has a bar tab going because he'll need it."

Jax smiled again, sweet and sexy enough to melt any resistance Arian might have left. "Hurry," he said to Penny, dropping his hand and pushing away from the doorframe.

Arian stepped aside on very wobbly legs. "Come inside."

He squeezed into the tiny hallway, his body brushing against hers, leaving a trail of fire in his wake. Arian shivered at the touch, and held the door open as Penny swept past. With a wink, she flipped the sign on the doorknob from 'service room' to 'do not disturb' and pulled the door closed behind her.

Arian stood staring at the emergency evacuation

procedures on the back of the room door. What now? She turned to see Jax out on the balcony, standing with his hands on the railing, staring out to sea. Taking a deep breath, she went to stand next to him. The silence stretched and Arian waited, her nerves fluttering like butterflies in her stomach.

"I'm really sorry about what happened at the cove today. Odys knows what buttons to press. It's an argument we've had for years."

"Yes, Penny has the same habit. I guess it comes from being friends since childhood."

He turned around and leaned back against the railing, one foot up against the trellis. His hand covered hers. "We fight like boys, I'm afraid, but we shake hands and forgive. It's a long story and I'd like to tell it to you. I need to explain, but I'm afraid to."

"Afraid? Why?" Arian wasn't sure anything he'd say would make sense right now anyway. Not when her nerve endings zapped and her hands itched to touch him. The smell of coconut lotion mixed with the muskiness of his cologne teased her nose and stirred the desire that simmered within her whenever he was near. She shivered.

"Because there is something about you that has touched my heart and I'm afraid if I tell you my secrets too soon, we will lose this magic between us." With a gentle tug, he pulled her towards him and into his arms. He tipped up her chin with a gentle finger. "I came here to talk, but when you're near, the world and reality fade and all I see is you."

His hand on her back massaged slow circles then his fingers danced up and down her spine. Arian relaxed in his hold and let the sensations warm her heart, though her mind still warred with what she'd seen and heard at the cove. "We've only just met."

"Yet I feel like I've known you forever. I tried to stay away, Arian. I know we scared you and Penny with our intensity. We are Greek, passionate and proud of our heritage. Sometimes we forget others don't know our story, nor do they believe in myths."

Arian felt the vibration of his voice under her hands, the intensity of his tone in her heart. For the first time since Gran died, she felt a part of something, a sense of belonging, a connection that ran deeper than anything she'd ever experienced, stronger even than her relationship with Gran.

"There is so much I need to tell you, so much to explain, and I need your trust before I can say anymore." He pressed a kiss to the top of her head as he held her against his heart.

"I don't trust easily, Jax. I've been hurt too many times trusting the wrong people." Yet in his arms, she felt safe, secure and loved. How could that happen so quickly?

"I understand. I too have difficulty trusting, but you, Arian … you appear to be an exception. When I am with you my heart soars and my spirits lift as if you are breathing new life into my soul. I understand how that may sound pathetically poetic. I swear on my honour, it's not a pick-up line."

She smiled into his shirtfront. If someone had said that to her in the bar last night, she wouldn't have had any trouble believing it was a pick-up line. Coming from Jax, it sounded like a promise of paradise. "I believe you because I feel the same."

"Good." Relief threaded his sigh. "May I please kiss you now?"

Too far under his spell to object, and captivated by the need in his eyes, she whispered, "Yes." The muscles in her abdomen tightened with expectation as he lowered his head. Arian rose on her toes, meeting him halfway.

His mouth brushed hers, softly, sweetly, until she leaned closer and stilled his lower lip with a nip. Any more teasing would drive her insane. With a soft growl, he crushed her to him and kissed her until she moaned with a mixture of pleasure, pain and desperation. Whatever magic this man possessed, she wanted it — all of it — now.

Her hands wandered up over his firm chest, across his shoulders and into the soft tangle of hair at his nape. The brush of his beard against her skin sent shivers of delight through her as his lips left hers to press a trail of kisses down her neck. She arched against him, feeling the press of his readiness against her stomach.

"Jax," she whispered against his ear.

"I swear I never came for more than to apologise ..." His hand traced a fiery trail down her spine, caressed the rounded curve of her hips and lifted her against him. "... but, so help me Zeus, I need you, Arian," he murmured and nibbled at the soft skin beneath her ear. "I want to feel your skin beneath my touch, adore you with my lips and make you mine. Not to own, but to share our own special Paradise."

Arian stretched against him, luxuriating in the feel of his hard body against hers. "Yes."

She whimpered as his fingers brushed the firmness of her breasts, begging for his touch. Then his hands were under her bottom, lifting her up as he moved away from the railing and into the room. She wrapped her legs around his waist, her fingers already busy at the buttons of his shirt. He lowered her to the bed and shrugged it off.

Arian admired him through a haze of desire. Warm bronzed skin stretched across the expanse of his chest, firm and oh so touchable. He closed the gap between them. Propped up on his elbows, he lay over her, stroking the hair away from her face. "Your hair is like spun gold mixed with a touch of sunset." Jax lifted the strands and let them fall through his fingers. "Your skin is like silk."

Each word stroked across her skin as he left a trail of kisses down her neck. Strong fingers moved to the ties of her bikini top. While he worked the bow free, she explored the contours of his chest with her fingertips. She smiled, insanely aroused at the sharp intake of breath as her nail traced the line of hair that arrowed south, stopping at the waistband of his shorts.

"Touch me, Arian. Make me yours."

Her top disappeared and his hands cupped her breasts lovingly. He pressed a kiss into the gentle valley between them. Nimble fingers tweaked and tortured her nipples until she surged against him.

Arian's fingers fumbled at the button of his shorts, weak with the need to do as he asked, as eager as he was to explore. The button snapped free and she drew the zipper down. Cupping her hand around him, she stroked from base to tip with a feather-light touch that had him pressing into her palm.

With a sigh that whispered across her lips, he touched his mouth to hers. His fingers trailed to her waist, caressing each curve until her nerve endings came alive to the sheer magic of his touch.

"There are things I cannot tell you yet," he said, his voice soft and soothing. "But I can show you some of it. Will you come with me, Arian?"

Arian's head spun with the sensations his fingertips created on her skin. She pushed his shorts down, caressing the curves of his hips, stroking the firm muscles of his buttocks. "Yes."

He kissed her then, a long, lingering kiss that began with the rub of his lips against hers. His tongue teased the seam until he parted it, dipping inside to stroke and curl around hers, angling his head to deepen the touch, drawing every ounce of her soul up and out, leaving Arian floating on a cloud of sensation.

Her hands stroked the corded muscles of his back, felt the rise and fall of his shoulders as his hands explored her body. She squirmed as his fingers found what they were looking for and whimpered as he dipped between the moist folds. Pleasure streaked through her at each light, teasing touch.

He eased off her bikini bottom and Arian sighed as the final barrier between them disappeared. His mouth left hers to follow a trail over her chin, down her throat, between her breasts, stopping for a brief moment further down so his tongue could dip into her navel, before continuing on its way to the ultimate destination.

Arian bit down on her lip to stem the scream that rose in her throat as his tongue stroked the wetness between her thighs and his teeth grazed her sensitised nub. She closed her eyes, captivated by the feel of his warm skin against her thighs and the brush of his lips against the folds of her womanhood.

Blindly, she sought his head with her hands,

entwining her fingers in his thick mane of hair, massaging his scalp in time with each stroke of his tongue. Lights flashed behind her eyelids as she felt the first vibrations of an orgasm shudder through her. "Jax," she cried out.

Jax lifted his head and made his way back up over her stomach, her skin alive with sensation. "Ahh, Arian," he sighed, "you taste like temptation."

Arian was beyond words as she untangled her hands from his hair to stroke down the back of his neck. He moved up over her, lowering his body until his skin, glistening with his own passion, touched hers. The graze of his chest against her hardened nipples almost sent her spiralling again.

"Hold on for me, my love," Jax whispered, as he bent his head to draw a pale pink bud into his mouth.

She heard the unmistakable rustle of a foil packet that kept his hands away from her body. Releasing her nipple, he straightened away from her. Arian opened her eyes to watch as Jax rose on his knees, looking every bit like a descendant of the gods with his desire-darkened eyes, moist lips and proud manhood. She admired the skill and ease with which he sheathed himself, her heart skipping a beat at the size of him.

He caught her watching and smiled. "Are you ready, my Faerie Queen?"

Arian had no words left. Instead she nodded and chewed her lip. He leaned forward and ran his thumb across her mouth. Eyes on his, she nibbled at the pad and thrilled in the sharp intake of breath and darkening of his eyes. Excitement raced through her at the intensity she saw there. The time for foreplay was over. She reached out to stroke the skin of his muscular thighs, up over the firm hips to his waist.

He shuddered and lowered himself over her. "Look at me, *agape mou.* I want to see your face, your eyes." He pressed against her, his caress warm and tender. "Let me love you the way you should be loved." With a gentle nudge, he entered her.

Arian squeezed her eyes shut at the rush of pleasure, the fullness of him inside her, and gave a brief thought to how right it felt before she gripped his thighs and urged him on. She opened her eyes. Still he held on, the effort it cost him evident in the sweat beading on his forehead. She raised a hand to stroke his face and squeezed her muscles around the length of him.

His breath hitched and she swore she heard his heart pounding out a tattoo. He retreated against the gentle pull of her muscles and when she released them, he slipped back in, only to repeat the process until Arian's nails dug into the cheeks of his buttocks and he couldn't hold the pace any longer. Arian had no complaints. He'd teased her for long enough. She pulled his head down to hers and kissed him with all the ferocity of a lioness on the hunt.

Together they rode the waves, the rise and fall of the climax, until Arian thought she'd die from the pleasure. As each fought and lost the desire for control, Arian cupped his cheek in her palm, stared deeply into his eyes and, with one final thrust, he gave her the promised glimpse of Paradise, a world so beautiful and filled with such wondrous sensations, she cried out at the wonder of it.

Arian sighed as she floated feather-light to Earth. Jax had left her briefly to use the bathroom, but he'd returned to take her in his arms and hold her against his side, stroking the skin on her arm where it lay across his firm stomach. Occasionally, she felt the loving reverence of his lips against her hair. He seemed simply content to hold her. No reaching for the television remote or leaving the bed for a beer. Arian pressed a kiss into his collarbone and settled more comfortably against him, her leg across his. She stroked her foot against his calf.

"What are you thinking?"

His chest rose and sank with a sigh under her ear. "About you, *agape mou*, and how lucky I am to have found you at last."

Arian smiled. "Oh, I think I'm the lucky one." She stretched against him with luxurious satisfaction.

He chuckled, the sound vibrating through her and stirring her body into desire again. That chuckle should be X-rated, she thought. Damned if Jax shouldn't come with a health warning because she thought she'd died in his arms. She'd never considered sex an adventure … until now.

"Want to hear the end of that story we started in the cove today? Then we should rescue Penny from Odys."

What she really wanted was to feel his hands on her again, loving her, taking her back to the Utopia she'd seen at the height of their passion, when she'd felt him pulsing inside her and wished there was nothing to stop his lifeblood from fusing with hers. In one tender moment, he'd fulfilled all of Arian's dreams and left her wanting more. But she'd settle for a story for now, if only to hear his voice and feel the rumble of it beneath her ear.

"I have a feeling she might not want to be rescued. Does the story have a happy ending?"

"I hope so, my love." He wriggled down until they were face to face. Lying with their heads close on the pillow and their hands clasped between them, Jax began his tale.

"After his death, Zeus exiled Ajax's soul to an island where he lived in Purgatory, the price he paid for dishonour. Taking his own life was cowardice in Zeus' mind. For centuries, Ajax wandered in search of a way to redeem his honour and prove to Zeus he was worthy of a second chance." He tucked stray wisps of Arian's hair behind her ear and pressed a kiss on her nose. "But it wasn't that simple. Zeus was adamant Ajax learn his lesson."

"What was the lesson he needed to learn?" Arian whispered into the space between them.

His eyes held hers and again she saw the sadness in them. "That life and love are far more important than wealth and possessions. The Shield of Achilles was more than mere magical protection in war, it represented strength of character and could only be won by the god strong enough to love unconditionally."

Arian shifted, closing the gap between them. "What happened then?"

"Zeus decided it was time for Ajax to return to life to find the answers. He would have to fight a battle for something far more precious than the shield."

Arian propped herself up on one elbow and watched his face, waiting for him to continue. This was more than a mythical tale to him, she realised. This was a passion that ran deep in his heart, more than taking pride in his Greek heritage. "Now I'm really intrigued. What could possibly be more valuable than the Shield of Achilles?"

He pulled her down on top of him, aligning her body with his, tucked her head under his chin and wrapped his arms around her tightly. "Ajax had to find The One who completed him as a man, the woman who would restore his belief in mankind, someone who believed in him enough to stop him from giving up on true happiness. You see, Zeus could give Ajax life, but only The One could give him back his heart and soul."

Arian pressed a kiss into his neck and sat up, straddling him. "That's beautiful, Jax. Did he find her … The One?"

His body stirred to life beneath her and she had no strength left to resist the urge to encourage his passion. She looked at his beautiful, sculptured face before she raised his hands to press her breasts into his palms. Each stroke of his thumbs across the flesh sent sparks of desire through her. Dampness grew between her thighs and she moved against the growing length beneath her.

His hands travelled down her skin, leaving a trail of excitement in their wake, until they settled at her hips. Eyes on his and a smile on her face, Arian reached between their bodies to guide him inside her. She paused for a moment, clenched her muscles around him and enjoyed the look of satisfaction on his face. With slow movements, she began to ride him with a rhythm he matched stroke for stroke. Arian gloried in the feel of him, the width and the length that completed her in a way that convinced her they were more than bed mates.

For a while there were no more words except for the murmured whispers of lovers and the united cry of fulfilment. Sated, Arian fell on Jax's chest, her breath coming in satisfied gasps. She felt the press of his lips to her temple as he whispered, "Yes, *agape mou*, only she found him and now he has to fight the battle to keep her."

Words were stupid things. Jax threw his arm up across his eyes and tried to block out the voice in his head that called him a liar. When he'd knocked at Arian's door, sex was the last thing on his mind. He'd planned to apologise … again … and weasel his way back into an easy friendship where he could do Zeus' bidding, serve and protect as instructed by Helen.

Then she'd opened the door looking so damned beautiful, fragile and hurt that it knocked him flat on his arse, and all he'd wanted to do was hold her and tell her the whole goddamn story of his miserable existence so she'd understand. But love didn't exist. Lust, yes, but not the happy-ever-after stuff. Zeus himself was a prime example that a man could no more stay faithful than a woman could. Hadn't Athena proved that one to be true, claiming to be madly in love with Odysseus yet flirting with Ajax at the same time?

He listened to Arian's breathing and felt the soft rise and fall of her breasts against him. Damned if it didn't feel like she belonged there, at his side, in his arms. What magic had she weaved around him? Was this another one of Athena's tricks? Another hallucination to drive him insane? He'd likely wake up on the beach somewhere with an armful of seaweed or some other cruel trick Athena would come up with.

No, this was worse than being baited by the toxic goddess. This reeked of one of Zeus' tests. One he'd failed by sleeping with the very woman he was meant to watch over. And didn't that make him a right bastard. This couldn't happen again, even though the fulfilment — the wholeness — was nothing like he'd ever experienced before. It was a big mistake and the only person to blame for this was himself, a mistake that could not only cost him his soul, but his heart and trust too. No, he needed to forget this magical coming together and concentrate on the true task, because he could not fail again.

CHAPTER FIVE

"It's about time the two of you showed up," Odys said later when Jax and Arian found them in the bar. "Penny's chewed my ear off and emptied my wallet on cocktails." He winced as Penny punched his shoulder.

"Someone had to free the moths, since you don't open it very often," she retorted. "You okay, Arian?"

"All good, Penny," she said, smiling up at Jax when he squeezed her hand.

Jax wished he could say the same. He felt … a complete lying, double-dealing jackass. When Zeus had said he'd find the Faerie Queen on Paradise Beach, he'd doubted the great god's sanity. A part of him wished she looked more like one of the hard-faced shrews Hades kept around his palace. That way he could remain immune to skin like silky peaches, hair spun with the golden glow of a sunset and eyes the colour of the grass on Mount Olympus.

The challenge was set. He would damn well keep her close until Zeus got his shit together. Then he'd leave and forget she ever existed with his heart and mind intact. He helped her up onto a bar stool and stood close as she chatted to Penny.

The exotic floral scent of her body wash tantalised his senses, bringing back the memory of her in the shower, the skin of her back cool against his chest as he'd lathered the liquid soap over every dip and curve, teased the peaks of her nipples and delighted in the clenching of her abdomen as he followed the trail that led to the place he wanted to enjoy most.

"Jax, for gods' sakes man, leave the women to their chatter and come over here." Odys glared at him from next to the jukebox.

Jax glared back. *Back off, Odys.*

You back off, Ajax, before you set the goddam bar alight.

Startled, Jax looked down at the hand he'd rested on the bar counter next to his beer. The wood beneath his palm glowed red. Quickly, he curled his fingers into his palm and shoved his hands in his pockets. He moved across the room to stand next to Odys. "Thanks for the heads up."

"Horny bastard," Odys said. "I sat here on tenterhooks waiting for the hotel fire alarms to go off while you two were up in the room. I'm pleased you were able to control your passion."

"I've learnt a few tricks since being in exile, Odysseus. A few thousand years is time enough to master the art of controlling the sparks."

"You weren't doing so well a moment ago. I'd stick close to water next time — perhaps keep to the shower, huh?" Odys grinned.

"Stay out of my thoughts, you dirty sonofabitch, and you won't get jealous."

This time Odys' laugh shook the walls. "Jealous? Not a chance. I had the lovely Penny to entertain me, although I might have to find an effective way to silence those sweet lips. She asked way too many questions thanks to her internet studies. It was pretty damn difficult to answer them without letting on we really were at the Battle of Troy."

"Yes, the more they become part of our lives, the harder it will become to hide the truth. How will we know when the time is right?"

Odys shrugged. "Who knows? Maybe we can talk to Helen. She's the one with direct access to the big man."

"Tomorrow we'll ask her. Is she joining us for dinner tonight?"

"Nah, she said she needs her beauty sleep. She seems to think she's going to need her full store of strength and patience in the near future."

Jax grinned. "We do test her patience, don't we?"

"That we do. Here come the girls now, let's have a bite to eat. Entertaining Penny is bloody hard work and I'm hungry."

"You always said you were looking for a woman who challenged you, Odys. I think you may have found her." Jax slapped his shoulder and they moved to meet the girls halfway. "Who's up for a picnic on the beach?"

"Ugh, haven't we had enough sand in our diet?" Penny grumbled.

"Oh come on, Penny, where's your sense of adventure? The moon is bright, the sea is calm and it's a lovely evening. We're only here for another few days before we have to go back to reality. Let's live a little. Besides, surely pure Greek sand is better than ingesting the exhaust fumes over Melbourne?" Arian slipped her arm through Penny's.

Jax's heart stopped beating. Oh bloody hell, that meant they'd be back on a darn plane again. Hades had the habit of ditching planes in the sea. If he knew who Arian was and that she'd be on the plane to Melbourne, he'd be suited up and flashing his pilot's license before they could saddle the harpies.

He tried to keep his voice calm and even as he asked, "When are you heading home?"

"On Friday."

Two days? That's all the time he had to come up with a plan? Would she still want to see him once she returned to her normal life? He'd have to come up with a damned good excuse to want to fly back with her and Penny, a reason to play the role of the enamoured lover. It was tempting to take a look at her thoughts but he resisted. Was she thinking about their interlude in the room? Had he really put that dreamy look in her eyes? His heart swelled with an emotion far too close to infatuation.

No, he wouldn't peek, no matter how tempted he was. Zeus had been perfectly clear on the rules — no cheating, no magic that might let on as to who or what he really was. So Jax reined in his godly powers as best he could. It would be so easy to simply place her under a spell and sweep her away to Olympus, but that wouldn't win her over or keep her safe and it sure wouldn't help his mission to redeem himself in Zeus' eyes.

"Jax?" Arian's sweet voice broke into his thoughts. "Should we ask the hotel to do up a picnic hamper for us?"

Her hand on his forearm chased away any

lingering thoughts of Zeus. Every time she touched him, he felt the bond grow stronger between them. Earning her trust was a good thing, right? "Yes, great idea. Odys, why don't you and Penny go on up and arrange that?"

Penny began to protest, but Odys cut her off. "Great idea. Trust me, Penny, if you see what Jax thinks is appropriate picnic fare, you'd be glad we're organising it." He led her away.

Jax took Arian's hand in his and they walked through the open doors of the bar onto the terrace. "Looking forward to going home?"

Arian shrugged. "I like it here, but I guess the holiday has to end sometime." She hesitated and turned to him. "Will you look me up when you get home?"

Did he have a choice? His fate lay in whatever the outcome was of the challenge he'd been set. If she took over the reign of Paradise successfully, he would be free to live in the modern world forever, his honour as a chieftain would be restored and peace would descend on the world once more. He should be excited about that, yet the future stretched before him filled with emptiness and a lifetime of meaningless wandering. No different really to what he had now.

He drew her closer and wrapped his arms around her waist. "Try and keep me away," he replied and prayed with all his heart he could keep that promise, if only to stave off the loneliness.

Two magical and fulfilling days later, Arian fought against the heaviness weighing on her chest and the sense of foreboding churning in her stomach.

"It's not goodbye, my beautiful Faerie Queen, only *kali antamosi*. Meet me at the airport when our flight comes in? We're on a flight out tomorrow."

Arian wiped a tear away from the corner of her eye and nodded. Right now, she couldn't trust her voice. He had come to mean so much in such a very short time. She would miss the warmth of his body next to hers, the comfort of his arms around her as they slept and the feel of his lips on hers.

Now, as their flight boarding call echoed through the cavernous airport building, Arian stood on her tiptoes to taste his mouth one last time. He took his time to kiss her thoroughly until her head spun and his image was burned into her mind. She felt his reluctance to let her go, but he did. Her hands slipped from his and she turned to follow Penny towards border control. Arian took one last look as they were ushered through. *I love you.*

I love you too.

"Come on, Arian. He's got your number," urged Penny. "Tomorrow he'll be breaking down the door of the apartment looking for you."

"I'm not so sure about that. I have this awful feeling that something bad is going to happen."

"Ignore it and think happy thoughts. You can entertain me all the way home with his awesomeness in bed."

"I am so not going to tell you every little detail," Arian laughed through her tears.

"Well, at least you'll have more to tell than me. As

sexy as Odys is, he didn't even try to make a move on me. I'm not even sure he really likes me that much."

"Don't be silly, Penny. What's not to like about you? Did you want him to make a move?"

"Nah, not really."

Arian laughed again. "Now you're lying."

Penny sighed. "Okay, maybe just a little. But I think there's something going on between him and Helen."

"What makes you say that?"

"Well, while you were cuddled up doing the horizontal rumba and setting off fire alarms all around Paradise Beach, Odys and Helen spent a lot of time huddled together on the boat."

"Really? Because I can tell you, Odys definitely had his eye on you … and the fire alarms were pure coincidence, by the way," Arian reassured her.

"Well, I guess we'll have to wait and see what happens when they return to Oakleigh."

They made their way up the ramp and onto the plane. Handing over their boarding passes, the hostess looked at them and smiled. "Ah, Miss Kendrick and Miss McKenna. We're happy to inform you that you've been upgraded to first class."

"Oh, wow," said Penny.

"Who ...?" began Arian. It could only be the work of Jax and Odys.

"A parting gift from our Greek boys?" Penny asked her as they followed the hostess towards the stairs leading to the upper floor of the plane.

"Who else could it be?"

"Well hell, then let's enjoy the luxury." Penny laughed. "I could get used to travelling like this."

"Far better than spending the next twenty-five hours in cattle class. I'll have to send Jax a text to thank him when we arrive home."

"Do you really think we'll see them again?"

Arian sunk into the comfort of her seat and clipped in her belt. "I hope so. We've done what we can to stay in touch — swapped details, made promises. Will you come with me to meet their flight, Penny?"

"I think you two swapped a lot more than just your contact details. And I'm not sure making promises while screaming *yes, yes, yes* in the heat of the moment counts," Penny teased. "Of course, I'll come with you. I wouldn't miss an opportunity to stir up the great god Odysseus." She chuckled.

Arian sighed. "It's too good to be true, Penny. I'm like a kid on a roller-coaster ride. It all happened so quickly. After what happened with Craig ..."

Penny took the in-flight blanket the hostess offered her and shook it out. "Hey, I'm not a big believer in love at first sight but let me tell you, Jax has it bad for you. Forget Craig, he's your past and that's where he belongs. It's time to look forward to the future. Stop overthinking and enjoy whatever comes next. What's the worst that can happen?"

CHAPTER SIX

A little fresher than normal thanks to the first class facilities, Arian and Penny arrived at Melbourne airport twenty-six hours later. The sense of foreboding grew and rattled at Arian's nerves. She shook it off as they checked in at border control. The flight had seemed like it would never end and not even their upgraded seats could take the edge off her mood. She missed Jax already, the warmth of his arms, the feel of his skin against hers.

In silence they waited at the carousel for their bags. Arian wondered what Jax was doing now. Was he down at the beach with Helen and Ermioni?

"Excuse me, Miss Kendrick?"

Arian turned to see a customs official behind her. "Yes?"

"Your bags have been taken care of and are waiting for you outside."

"Oh." Confused, she looked at Penny who shrugged. "Are Penny's there too?"

"Yes, now, if you'll follow me?"

Arian's heart skipped a beat. Had they found something illegal in her luggage? She visualised the contents of her suitcase and ruled out her Greek purchases. No wood, no fruit or food, and she'd declared her duty free shopping. With a puzzled look at each other, they followed the officer out of the crowd fighting to reach their luggage.

Instead of leading them into the customs hall as Arian had expected, he took them down a long corridor and out through the doors into the arrivals hall. As the doors slid open silently, the foreboding Arian battled in her tight chest sank to clench at her stomach. Cameras flashed and an excited buzz filled the hall. Reporters called out questions she had no answer for. Her eyes adjusted to the artificial lighting supplied by the television camera crews.

"What the hell is going on, Arian?" Penny hooked an arm through hers.

"I don't know. I have a really, really bad feeling about this ..."

Panic clamped her mouth shut as she spotted Craig's football mates huddled with their WAGs near the door leading out of the terminal. *Uh-oh.* The press, his entourage, his fans ... that could only mean—Craig swept her up in his arms against his muscular chest and swung her in a circle. Cameras flashed as applause and cheers broke out. She looked down to see his face a little below her chin.

"I've missed you, Arian," he said loudly, before letting her slide down his professional-football-player's chest. "I have something really important to say."

"Uh-oh, now *I've* got a bad feeling about this." Penny looked from Craig to Arian.

Arian tried to wriggle out of his hold, but he tightened

it. Anger warred with embarrassment as she pushed against his chest, nausea rising rapidly in the wake of panic.

"Arian Kendrick, will you marry me?"

The crowd roared with excitement, setting off the cameras again. Craig kissed her, slowly, tenderly and far too familiarly for someone who had dumped her only a month before. His kisses used to stir her into passion, set her blood on fire. Now they left her cold. She tore her lips from his and glared at him. "What the hell do you think you're doing?" she whispered angrily.

He placed his lips to her ear. "Play along. I'll explain later."

"I will not play along. Whatever it is you've cooked up, forget it. Let me go right now." She pushed hard against his chest. The crowd heckled and teased at her resistance.

"You're making a fool of me." Craig's arms tightened around her.

"You do that quite successfully without my help."

"I made a mistake. Please forgive me. I can't bear to be without you anymore," he begged loudly then whispered, "For God's sake, play along so I can get us out of here before you make it worse."

Arian opened her mouth to speak, but the pleading look in his eyes made her close it again. He'd better have a damn good reason for pulling this move and she couldn't wait to hear it.

Slipping an arm around her shoulders, he waved to the crowd as he moved her towards the exit. "Sorry, folks," he said as reporters waved their microphones at him, "I'm sure you can understand we have a lot to talk about and some making up to do." He winked suggestively at the cameras.

The good-natured ribbing of his teammates followed them out the door and to the waiting limousine. As he dragged her towards it, Arian looked back at the pavement where Penny stood abandoned in the crowd. "What about Penny?"

"Simon will make sure she gets home okay."

"Craig ..." It took all Arian's self-control not to yell. She dug her heels in against his insistent tugging. "You'd better have a damn good explanation for this. Simon will be lucky if *he* gets home in one piece. Penny's ready to rip him a new arsehole after his behaviour at the same after-party where *you* slept with the coach's daughter. What kind of game are you two playing this time?"

"Save it, Arian. I'm not in the mood."

"Oh, *you're* not in the mood? I've just flown across the world to be met by the boyfriend —"

"Fiancé."

"— *ex-boyfriend* who dumped me, then proposes to me in some stupidly concocted publicity stunt and *you're* not in the mood?"

"I upgraded you to first class, didn't I? Good God, I haven't even put the goddamn ring on your finger yet and already you're nagging like a fishwife," Craig snarled.

The crack of Arian's palm against Craig's cheek echoed through the crowd, stunning the media chatter into silence. Cameramen and reporters surged forward, the scent of a real story stronger than a romance as Craig wiped a drop of blood off his lip. Arian stepped back from the limousine.

"Naff off, Craig. I'm not in the mood to play your

stupid games. It was over the moment you willingly hopped into the sack with someone else." She turned and moved to where Penny had pushed their baggage cart away from the whispering crowd. "Come, Penny, let's go home."

They walked away towards the taxi rank, ignoring the uproar behind them. Her palm stung and her heart pulsed erratically in her chest. A month ago she would have been over the moon if Craig had proposed. Now it left her cold and empty. She should have stayed in Mykonos.

Hades rubbed his cheek. Okay, so maybe posing as the Faerie Queen's football star ex-boyfriend wasn't such a good idea after all. Bloody little hellion. If he didn't want her queendom so damn much, he'd have sent her straight to his dungeon where he'd torture the little hellcat into submission with whips and chains.

He heaved a sigh. How had such a brilliant plan gone so wrong? It should have been easy. Sweep her off her feet, put her in the limo, take her to Paradise, get her sworn in to the throne and marry the bitch so he'd be king. A year or two — give or take — would be enough time to win over the inhabitants to the dark side, then she could die mysteriously in her sleep and Paradise would be his.

And he'd gone to so much trouble to make sure Ajax the Not-So-Great and his entourage couldn't be on the same flight. It cost him a fortune getting all those exiles on the plane to fill up the seats. Fake passports were damn hard to come by, with all the best forgers living it up in the courtyards of hell. With such short notice, he'd had to use some two-bit thief who'd extorted a ridiculous amount of euros from his pockets. There'd be a special reservation downstairs for him very soon.

Never mind. Tomorrow was another day and there was enough time to hatch a new scheme. Two for the price of one … bargain.

Jax reared up in bed, his cheek stinging and pulse racing. *Arian.* The remnants of the dream he'd had remained, burned into his mind's eye. He'd seen Arian slipping away from him, being drawn into the deep, dark shadows of a place where he could no longer reach her. With each fading glimpse, he thought he felt his soul die a little. Premonitions sucked … big time.

He pushed the too heavy covers away from his naked body and swung his feet to the floor. Raking a hand through his hair, he stood then pushed aside the heavy drapes—a perfect day on Paradise Beach except for the storm brewing on the horizon. Angry black clouds gathered and lightning spiked in the distance. The sign of trouble afoot, for sure.

"Jax, open up," called Odys, hammering on the door, shaking it in the frame.

With a sigh, Jax grabbed his boxers and stepped into them. "Hold your horses, Odysseus." He walked over and unbolted the door. "What's up?"

"Zeus wants a word with you up in Helen's room."

"He's here?" Jax shivered. If the big man had come all the way to Mykonos to see him, he'd be in deeper shit than he was already.

"No, but he's not happy, in case you haven't noticed the storm he's kicked up. Here —" Odys pushed into the room and grabbed a t-shirt from the foot of Jax's bed, "— put this on and get your butt upstairs."

With a sigh of relief, Jax slipped the t-shirt on and followed Odys out the room and to the lift. Two floors later, they pushed through the lift doors into the corridor leading to Helen's room. The door stood ajar and Jax could hear Helen's soothing voice. Thunder crashed outside, shaking the windows.

"Ajax is here now, Zeus," Helen said, turning around, her mobile phone clenched to her ear, knuckles white.

Jax cast Odys a resigned look and shook his head. *This is bad, very bad.* Lightning struck so close to the window that all three immortals jumped back. Helen handed the phone to Jax.

"Zeus." Jax pinched the bridge of his nose, feeling a headache begin to pulse behind his eyes.

"You're a fool, Ajax the Great." Zeus' voice boomed down the line and bounced off his eardrum to echo in his head. God knows why Zeus bothered with the phone when Jax was sure he could be heard all the way from Mount Olympus, irrespective of the sonic boom of the storm he brewed. "You know how I hate bloody modern technology, yet you force me to use this … this unreliable device with its lousy reception because showing up down there to beat the snot out of you would cause a goddam riot."

What could he say to that? "Yes, sir. I'm sorry."

"Do you have any idea how many software updates I had to go through to make this connection work? Five. Five, I tell you."

Jax held the phone a little further away from his ear

and waited for his punishment to be handed out. He wondered if Zeus realised how hot the phone was getting with all that anger radiating through it.

"I hand you the queen, neatly packaged, all wrapped up like a newborn in a blanket, and you let her slip through your fingers."

"We couldn't get on the plane, it was full. I have her number. I'm looking her up when we get back to Melbourne. We're only a day behind them."

This time the phone almost ripped from his hand as Zeus roared in unison with the thunder.

"Idiot. Trusting Earth's medieval technology will cost you your *soul.*" Lightning flashed inside the room, scorching the bedspread on the king-size bed. A newspaper bounced onto the pillow, front page up. "You should never have let her go back alone. You blew it. You delivered her right into the hands of your enemy."

Jax picked up the paper, avoiding the smoking, singed edges. Mistake … he'd made a big mistake, and if his brains and balls hadn't been so baffled by her beauty and enticing body, he would have seen this for the set-up it was.

Cold dread and shame travelled up from his feet, curdled his stomach and encased his heart in ice. There on the front page was Arian, wrapped in the arms of a blond, muscular, athletic type with the headlines proclaiming a match made in heaven. The newspaper fluttered from his nerveless fingers.

Odys picked it up and read aloud. "Football superstar Craig McMahon attempted to prove today that absence does make the heart grow fonder. All bets were off on whether the wedding of the year between McMahon and

Arian Kendrick would take place or not when an away game this year ended with him in bed with the coach's daughter. After a month apart, Kendrick returned from licking her wounds in Mykonos to find McMahon at the airport, hat in hand and armed with an eight-carat diamond. Could it be the Bachelor of the Year candidate, McMahon, will be off the market after all? How could Kendrick refuse — hey!"

Jax ripped the paper from Odys' hands and tossed it out through the open sliding door and over the balcony. Lightning struck the newspaper and it littered the pavement below with confetti.

"Fix it, Polemistis," boomed Zeus. "Before I forget my forgiving nature and send you back to Purgatory where your soul will wander until Hades comes for you, and your chance to restore your honour will be lost *forever.*"

The line went dead and the storm cleared, leaving a pristine sky in its wake. Jax handed the phone to Helen and sunk onto the edge of the singed mattress. Pain squeezed at his heart and panic tore at his gut. If he lost Arian, he'd die. He couldn't bear the thought of spending a lifetime at the right hand of Hades. The demon thought sulphur was an aftershave, for gods' sake.

"I've changed our flights. A car will pick us up in an hour to take us to the airport. Go and get ready, Jax. There's no time to waste." Helen laid a gentle hand on his shoulder.

He stood, letting her hand slip down his biceps and come to rest on his forearm. "Yes, no time to waste." Right now, he wasn't sure which hurt the most, his head or his heart. Goddammit, he should have asked her to stay, to travel back with him instead.

"I'll go and get the bags, Helen. And some clothes for Jax. We don't want him giving everyone a heart attack in those boxers. Give him a shot of ouzo. He's looking a little worse for wear."

Jax sat on the carpet with his back against the bed, head in his hands, his mind filled with all the things he could have done to stop her leaving. Ermioni crawled into his lap and touched his face with a chubby, sticky hand. He wrapped his arms around the little girl and cuddled her close.

"Ermioni loves Jax," she said.

Jax smiled sadly. "And I love you too, Ermioni."

"Ermioni likes pretty lady." Her big blue eyes stared deeply into his.

He pressed a kiss into her mop of curly blonde hair. "I like her too, little one."

She wriggled out of his arms and stood to hold out her hand to him. "Come," she said, "find pretty lady."

Jax closed his massive hand around her tiny one and felt the power in her she hadn't learnt to use yet. The little magic she did know showed him a glimpse of Arian looking very angry, standing at the edge of the shadows he'd seen in his dream. He hadn't lost her yet.

Arian seethed as the taxi driver unloaded their luggage outside their apartment building. Pulling in behind them, the Channel Twelve media van doors banged open, and a reporter and cameraman fell over each other in their haste to nab an interview.

"Miss Kendrick … How do you feel about turning

down football's most eligible bachelor? What are your thoughts on his affair with the coach's daughter? Do you feel betrayed?"

Penny rolled her eyes as she swung her bag over her shoulder, almost knocking the microphone out of the reporter's hand. "Miss Kendrick has no comment," she said.

"Who are you?" The reporter scrambled to save the microphone from falling onto the brick pavers outside the South Yarra apartment block.

"None of your business."

"Miss Kendrick, will you reconsider Craig McMahon's proposal? Could it be you're jet-lagged and not thinking things through? You've turned down a man women are lining up to marry. Has his proposal taken you by surprise?"

So many smart-arsed responses sprang to Arian's lips. She bit them back. The only smart-arse this whole bizarre soap opera needed was Craig. All she wanted was peace and quiet to think. What possible motive could Craig have for pulling this stunt? Except, of course, to save his butt. She swiped her security card in the lock, pushed open the door and hurled her cases into the lobby. Penny pushed it closed on the reporter, his crew and the gathering crowd.

"Home," breathed Arian. She eyed the row of letterboxes on the wall, found their apartment number and pulled the overflow of mail from the slot. Tossing it into her bag, she turned to Penny. "Thanks."

"For what?"

"For being there to rescue me."

Penny shrugged. "Craig is still a dickhead. Nothing's changed since we've been away. Still thinks he's the next bloody star just because he's been voted in for *Cleo's* Bachelor of the Year. You'll feel better after a shower and a nap."

Arian felt Penny's hand on her arm as they took a left around the corner to where the lift waited to whisk her up to the cool, air-conditioned luxury of their shared apartment. She looked out on the spectacular view of Melbourne from the glass capsule as it raced up to the sixth floor. The glitter of lights on the horizon normally relaxed her, but tonight her thoughts were on the reporter and his crew fast becoming annoying specks of trouble beneath her feet.

"You still pack a punch, Arian," said Penny as the lift doors swished open and they tumbled out with their luggage. "I reckon he's going to have a sore cheek for a while."

"What is this about, Penny? Has the coach's daughter thrown him over already, do you think?" Arian searched her handbag for the front door key.

"Either that or he's trying to save face … or he's been dumped from the selectors' panel for next season. No matter how hard the board tried, they couldn't keep the news out of the press that they'd found drugs in Craig's locker and he'd failed his urine test."

"True. That's what happens when you mess with the coach's daughter. Coach Bennett lost his job, his daughter's been exposed to a scandal of sex, drugs and alcohol. He's bound to be out for blood." Arian shrugged the sense of impending doom. If only they'd stayed a little longer, they could have flown back with Jax and the others. Although she doubted that would have changed anything.

"What a bloody mess." Penny pushed open the door and wheeled her suitcase inside. "I think a glass of wine is in order. That flight was long even in the luxury of first class."

"Now you're talking. I could do with one after that fiasco. Damn Craig to hell. He always has to have the last word," she muttered as she made her way to her bedroom.

Arian scattered the clothing from her suitcase onto her bed. Craig was such an arsehole when he wanted to be, pulling that stupid stunt at the airport, throwing her into confusion and mayhem, the bastard.

"I'm a total fool," she told the vanilla-coloured walls.

Was she being a fool over Jax too? Nervousness bubbled up her throat. Would Jax even bother with her when he got back? She pushed the doubts down. No point in dwelling on what ifs. She searched the contents of her handbag for her phone. Lipstick and a tube of sunscreen landed on top of her passport, followed by the sleep mask the air hostess had handed her shortly after take-off. She dug the mobile out from between a sales docket and a tourist map. Had he tried to contact her since they'd left Mykonos?

Pressing the silver button on the edge of the unit, she realised she hadn't had time to turn it on between being swept through customs and having her feet knocked out from under her by Craig. The screen remained stubbornly blank. That's what happens when you forget to charge the battery, Arian thought as she plugged the lead into the wall socket.

In the kitchen, the house phone rang but she ignored it. Vaguely she heard Penny telling the caller to "rack off". News-mongering journalists — perhaps if she ignored them for long enough they'd go away. Let them hound Craig and his bloody sponsors instead. The more she stayed out of it, the easier it would be to melt back into the shadows and out of the picture. With a sigh, she tossed the heap of clothes into the laundry basket and raked a frustrated hand through her hair.

Arian walked out of her room and into the miniscule kitchen where Penny had put a chilled bottle of wine on the counter. What was Jax doing now? She closed her eyes and concentrated hard. His face shimmered into view, but all she saw was his smile as he'd waved her goodbye at the airport.

Penny swept into the kitchen. "Hey, look at this. I picked up the paper someone left in the taxi and look who's on the front page … go figure." She handed Arian the folded newspaper, reached for the bottle of Swan Valley Classic White and poured them each a generous helping.

In big black letters, the headline screamed *Dastardly Demon Deeds* and underneath it, *Football's star Demon, Craig McMahon, is in hot water over drug allegations as the Demon Dodgers reconsider their line up for next season. McMahon, a nominee in this year's* Cleo *Bachelor of the Year contest, is said to be in a downward spiral after split from girlfriend Arian Kendrick, and the scandal that rocked the football community over his affair with Coach Bennett's daughter. Read the full story on page two.*

"Serves the bastard right."

Penny pulled a packet of crackers from the pantry cupboard, opened it and dipped one into her glass of wine. "Too right, mate. I guess that's the reason for the media hoo-ha at the airport?"

"He needs to show some remorse or respectability to stay on the team, I guess."

"So he ambushes you at the airport, and … what? Pretends everything is hunky dory Down Under?" She sucked on the damp end of the cracker, closing her eyes as it disintegrated in her mouth. "That's a bloody good wine."

"You can tell it's a good wine when it's soaked through a cracker? Sounds like a waste of wine to me. If the board's trying to cover up the scandal and smooth things over with the club, he might need a fiancée in time for the charity game on Saturday."

Penny stopped mid-sip and looked up. "The salt in the cracker enhances the flavour, and Craig is a fool," she said, swallowing the wine. "What the hell was he thinking pulling that stunt? Let him dodge his own demons for once. Pardon the pun." The plastic wrapper rattled as she pulled another cracker from the box. "What about Jax, the Almighty Greek and the allusions of Paradise? Has he tried to get a hold of you?"

Arian admired the colour of the classic white and focused on the bubbles caressing the glass. She downed the wine and allowed her head to spin in response to the taste of alcohol on her tongue. Maybe if she stayed drunk today, things would look rosier in the morning. Tears pricked her eyelids, a response to the mix of jet lag and wine.

"I don't know yet. It was good while it lasted but was it the real thing? I'm so confused right now. What if it was simply a holiday fling for him? It all happened so quickly …"

"Time will tell. You have — what? ... twenty-four hours, give or take — to wait for a reunion." Penny leaned over the counter and patted Arian's hand. "Don't write him off yet, okay?"

Arian propped up her chin in her hand, elbow on the table. "I don't know. What if there isn't a message from him?"

"Will you be devastated?"

Arian thought about Jax, the feel of his skin on hers, the intensity and passion in his eyes, the gentle stroke of his hands and the magical words he'd whispered between them. "Shattered. What am I going to do, Penny?"

"About whom … Craig or Jax?"

Arian's sigh echoed around the room. "Both, I guess."

The sound of glass against glass tinkled between them as Penny topped up their glasses. "Right, let's put this in perspective before those crackers soak up the wine. Which one should we dissect first — Craig or Jax?"

The liquid swirled in Arian's glass as she turned it in circles on the bare counter top, her mind miles away from Melbourne. "Huh?"

"Jeez, stay with me here, hon. Which one do you want to talk about next — Jax or Craig?"

"I don't know. It shouldn't be complicated but it is. I am so attracted to Jax, but I don't know if I'll ever see him again."

It was Penny's turn to sigh loudly. "Listen up, my lady Arian. When you and Jax are together sparks fly, fire alarms go off, you see heaven in his kiss and God knows what in his bed — you still need to tell me about that, by the way. What did you feel when you saw Craig again?"

Arian swallowed a sip of her wine. "Nothing ... absolutely nothing …"

"He's a cheating bastard. He doesn't deserve you."

"No, you're right, he doesn't. I just have this nagging voice in my head that I should give him another chance." A voice that filled her with apprehension not guilt, repulsion rather than allure … no, she'd come too far to turn back now. The only way was forward.

"Well, bloody ignore it. You'd be crazy to go back to that snivelling little bastard, and I know you're anything but crazy. You know he'll drop you faster than a slippery ball on a muddy field as soon as some groupie waves at him through the goalpost. Wait for Jax to find you." Penny reached across and squeezed Arian's hand. "He will find you. When he looks at you, his face lights up and even I can hear his heart pounding. Then I look at you and see those feelings mirrored on your face, and I know you're meant for each other."

Arian laughed, the combination of wine, jet lag and emotion making her head spin. "Oh my God, *Penny*, you're going all soft and gooey on me."

"Maybe … or maybe I have an ulterior motive."

"And what would that be?"

"I need you to find Jax so I can see Odys again. I rather liked riling him. We had fun with them, didn't we?"

Arian nodded and smiled vaguely. "Yes, it was fun. You're right, if Craig persists with this nonsense, I'll tell him to get lost. When my phone's charged, I'll send Jax a text to see how he's doing. Thanks, Penny. Where would I be without you?"

Penny grinned. "Halfway to paradise?"

CHAPTER SEVEN

Jax tried dialling Arian's number before boarding their flight but got no response. It went directly to voicemail. He left a message and hung up, switching off his phone in preparation for the flight. She was probably sleeping, exhausted after the flight. He could picture her in his bed. The soft fall of her lashes against her flushed cheeks, the little pout of her lips as she breathed, the warmth of her body snuggled into his. The vision had his heartbeat racing and his body hardening. Sex — he couldn't let it be more than that. His heart and mind were dedicated to being the greatest of all chieftains in Zeus' army. No woman would ever own his heart or mind again. Not even a beautiful Faerie Queen...

Surely the newspapers had it wrong. The media sensationalised everything when celebrities or sports stars were involved. Yes, it had to be a misunderstanding, the truth lost in translation by the Greek newspapers.

"Don't know why Zeus couldn't have teleported us. What's the point of being a god when we still have to use airplanes?" Odys grumbled as he stuffed their hand luggage into the gaps left in the overhead compartments.

"Stop whining, Odys. I doubt he'd want to attract any more attention after that storm today. It's all over the news about the unseasonal weather."

"Well, he could at least have let us fly first class. Economy seats weren't made for two great hulking blokes like us." He leaned heavily against Jax as he searched for the lock-in end of his seat belt. "Ermioni, *glykó mou*, wouldn't you like to swap seats and sit next to Grumpy *Theio* here? Your company might cheer him up a little."

Helen shot Odys a warning look while Jax stared aimlessly out the square window, ignoring them both. He simply didn't care that his friends had tried to cheer him up, distract him with their friendly hedging. In the place where his heart once pounded an icy hole had formed, as deep, dark and cold as the water well in the Enchanted Garden.

"Jax?" He felt the light touch of Helen's hand on his where he gripped the back of her seat, knuckles white. "Can Ermioni sit with you, so Odys the Whiner has more space to fidget for twenty-six hours?"

"Sure." No matter how much his heart hurt, he couldn't deny himself little Ermioni's company. Rather an aching heart than a sore head, which he would undoubtedly have if Odys whined all the way home to Melbourne.

He opened his arms to the warm bundle of ruffled skirts, picked up Ermioni and plopped her into the seat next to him. As he secured her into her belt, she planted a sticky kiss on his cheek and grinned. He smiled back as she gripped his cheeks with chubby hands and stared deep into his eyes.

In his mind he saw Arian, a wispy figure with sad eyes, standing with a man built for a forward and hands big enough to grip the slippery leather of a football. There was no happiness between them, only agitation. Craig McMahon's heart was no bigger than a ferret's but his ego blossomed over his aura. For that, Jax was glad. Surely Arian could never love a man who loved himself more than anything else in the world? Her voice whispered through his mind. *Jax ...*

"Thank you, Ermioni, precious child." The vision she'd sent him melted the ice around his heart a little and allowed hope to take root. She blew him a wet raspberry and hugged her blanket closer.

He sat back in his seat and waited as the engines of the Boeing A380 powered up beneath his feet. In a little over a day, he'd be home and one step closer to freedom. The thought should have cheered him up, instead it left a hollow in his gut.

Arian heard the chirp of her phone as she headed for her bedroom for a nap. The combination of jet lag and wine had taken their toll. She sighed. Two voicemail messages but no text message from Jax. Her heart tugged as she dialled in to her voice mailbox and listened to the dull, expressionless tone of the mailbox host. *You have ... two ... new voice messages*.

With a hitch in her breathing, she followed the prompts to play the first message. Her pulse raced as Jax's voice played soft and smooth as velvet against her ear. "My precious Arian, you haven't even boarded the plane yet and I miss you so much already."

She blamed the tiredness and wine for the tear that escaped her lashes and ran down her cheek as she played the second message. Jax again. This time he sounded out of breath, his tone urgent. "I saw the football player's proposal in the papers. I'm coming home on the next flight out. Please, Arian … wait for me."

Thank God she'd told Craig to rack off.

With little Ermioni asleep on the seat beside him, Jax unfolded the newspaper the hostess had handed out. His heart skipped a beat as he saw the photo on the front page. There was Arian with Craig McMahon, and the shot showed the moment her hand connected with his cheek. His Arian — tough, tetchy warrior queen — had caused media outrage. Zeus would have a fit at the attention the story was getting, but Jax couldn't help enjoying a little chuckle at her rejection of the arrogant football player.

Given the Boot, shouted the headlines. *Fears for football stud Craig McMahon's future with the Demons as his marriage proposal to long-time girlfriend, Arian Kendrick, gets the backhand.*

"Better her boot up his arse than mine," he muttered. He felt the back of his seat dip as Odys leaned over to see what he was reading.

"Hey, Grumpy, talking to yourself now?"

Jax chuckled and handed Odys the paper. "Looks like Zeus was worried about nothing after all."

The paper rustled as Odys sat back and shook it out. Jax unclipped his seatbelt and turned to lean over the back of the seat. Peering over, he watched his friend read the article.

"Clever girl," murmured Odys. "Uh-oh ..."

"Uh-oh what?"

He looked up, his face grim. "According to this, he's not giving up on her. *McMahon plans to embark on a crusade to win back the heart of his princess. According to the Demons' star forward, if his skill with a ball is as good as his romancing, Arian Kendrick will be a bride by June.* What a tool." He looked up at Jax again. "Mate, I do believe this is your call to arms. Let the battle begin."

CHAPTER EIGHT

The smell of toast and Vegemite wafted under her nose and Arian buried her face in her pillow. Jet lag fuelled exhaustion weighed her eyelids down as she fought off the remnants of sleep.

"Come on, princess. Time to rise and shine. You're trending." Penny's cheerful voice chased away the tail end of a delicious dream involving one sexy Greek god whisking her away to Paradise. "I brought you breakfast."

Arian groaned and rolled over as the mattress dipped. "What do you mean I'm trending?"

"Twitter. *#icequeen #heartbreaker*. Craig's Facebook post has reached one million hits already. Social media has gone into meltdown."

"Ugh. Are you serious? What did he post?"

Penny propped her laptop up on the pillow next to Arian's head and clicked on Craig's status. Arian squinted against the glare and read. *You're breaking my heart Arian Kendrick. Please say yes.*

Penny munched on her toast as Arian read the

comments under his status. "I like the one that says you're a mean witch and should be burnt at the stake," she said.

"That's not even funny, Penny, some of these fans take this shit seriously. Next thing you know I'll be getting hate mail." She pushed herself up and closed the laptop. "I'm going to kill him."

Penny snorted. "Imagine the hits that will get."

"Five hundred and twenty-two comments." Arian shook her head. "I have to check flights. Jax is coming home on the first flight out." She nudged Penny off the bed with her foot and pulled back the covers.

"There's one arriving via Abu Dhabi at 10:20 tonight. They're on it."

"Do you sleep with your laptop under your pillow?" Arian grumbled. "How did you even know to look for flights? Wait a minute, were you eavesdropping?"

"Nope, got a text from Odys with the flight number." Penny grinned. "Jax saw the article about the proposal in the paper. You're international news, baby."

Arian shuddered. "Great. Now every national *and* international newshound will be sniffing around my feet. I won't be able to pee without falling over them. What's the time?"

Penny looked at her watch. "Eleven. We've got a few hours to kill yet." She stood, taking the plate piled high with toast crusts with her. "Don't go outside, by the way. The media is camped on the pavement."

"Great, just … great. Hey, Penny?"

"Yeah?"

"I thought that toast was my breakfast?" Arian pointed at the plate.

"Oh ..." Penny grinned. "Guess you'll have to make

more then," she said, sweeping out the room and closing the door behind her.

Alone with her thoughts on how she would murder one arrogant football player and hide the body, Arian picked up the remote and turned on the television mounted in the corner on her bedroom wall. Channel Twelve's breakfast show hosts filled the screen looking disgustingly cheerful and groomed so early in the morning.

Arian wondered who'd dressed Amanda Dhiaga this morning. A salmon pink dress with frilly sleeves clashed with her too yellow spray-on tan. God, she wished the wardrobe department would think about it before they dressed TV hosts.

Worse was the newsfeed in the red banner that rolled across the screen. *Fans in uproar over Arian Kendrick's dumping of Demons Dodger, Craig McMahon. Football's bigwigs reconsider McMahon's future in football. Concerns for his ability to focus on training for Saturday's charity match.*

Seriously? The camera focused in on Mal Sebastian's once handsome face. The veteran host appeared to be losing his battle with Botox. His voice was still as smooth as velvet though, as he introduced his guests on the couch.

"Well … social media has gone into meltdown overnight about Craig McMahon's failure to win back his long-time love, Arian Kendrick."

Arian muttered, "Two years is a long time? Since when?"

"Not only are his fans up in arms, the team WAGs have come out in his defence too," Mal continued. "Hash tag SaveCraigM has trended at number one since last night in what the WAGs are calling their Twitterfit. Merlene, please explain, what exactly is a Twitterfit?"

Surprise, surprise. Princess Merlene front and centre fighting for her man, not wasting an opportunity to grab the spotlight. Tempted to turn off the telly, Arian forced herself to watch as her day got infinitely worse. The camera panned to the couch and there sat her nemesis with her gang of go-getters.

A headache spreading at her temples, Arian left them to talk to an empty bedroom and stepped into her bathroom for a shower.

Jax set his watch to Melbourne time as the captain announced to prepare for landing. Would Arian be waiting for him? He prayed for Zeus' kindness she would. Nervously, he chewed on his lip as he checked his seatbelt and Ermioni's, making sure they were secured. The plane began its descent and the hostesses made their final sweep of the cabin. Jax's heart rate soared as he took in the view of Melbourne spread beneath the belly of the Boeing. Down there somewhere was the woman who made him whole, the one who would redeem him from hell and give him something to live for. All he had to do was hope he could find her in the crowded terminal.

Tyres screeched as the wheels of the plane touched the tarmac with a bump and the G-force of the pilot adjusting the flaps to slow the big bird down jerked them forward in their seats.

"Bloody hell," grumbled Odys from the seat behind. "This boy needs a lesson in gentle landing."

"Be quiet, Odys. The landing wouldn't have been any softer if Zeus had transported us," Helen scolded. "He would likely have tossed you both out of the clouds on your stubborn backsides."

Jax sighed as the two argued lightly while the plane taxied to a standstill in front of the terminal building. All he wanted was to get out of this toothpaste tube they called an airplane and find Arian. He released his belt and stood up to haul bags out of the overhead locker, dumping Odys' in his lap and handing Helen hers. He dropped his on his seat, leaned over and hoisted the sleeping Ermioni up into his arms, cuddling her close, tapping his foot impatiently as people began to rise from their seats and clog the pathway to the exit portals.

His stomach churned and knotted in turns, and his jaw ached from clenching his teeth. Impatience boiled to the surface. He pushed it down, breathing slowly in through his nose, out through his mouth. He focused on the memory of Arian's sweet, calm face and felt the tension seep out of him as he breathed. She had to be there or there was no reason to live.

"C'mon, Big Boy, aisle's clear. Let's go." Odys nudged him in the ribs. Still balancing Ermioni, he swung his bag over his shoulder, narrowly missing making contact with Odys' chest. "Watch it," growled Odys.

Jax ignored him. No matter what mode of transport they chose, Odys never travelled well. Then again, on a man-made transport vehicle, none of them did. He strode purposefully towards the exit, the others following closely behind him.

Border control was a breeze but the arrival of a flight from Thailand just before them delayed the procession through customs. Officials seized a mother lode of excess cigarettes, undeclared foodstuff and other concealed items, interrogating passengers and handing out hefty fines. Interpreters scrambled between X-ray machines and inspection tables, while white-gloved officers handed out tissues to dry tears.

Jax hitched Ermioni up higher and swapped her from his left to the right, each moment of the wait eating away at his patience. How long would Arian wait? He looked at his watch. Half an hour ticked by with agonising slowness and the queue only moved a couple of feet. Relief flooded him as a customs official approached them.

"Passengers Polemistis, Laertiades, and Tyndareus?" He looked at them for confirmation. "Come with me, please. You have express check out passes."

Jax let out a breath of relief. Thank you, Zeus. He put Ermioni down, now awake and sucking her thumb, and she clasped Helen's hand as they followed the man out into the arrivals hall, bypassing all the weary passengers waiting in the queue. The doors swished open on a crowd blessedly thinned by the delay in customs and there she was … Arian, his beautiful, ethereal Faerie Queen with her head held high as she stood on tiptoe, stretching to see beyond the doors. Jax dropped his bag and ignored Odys' curse as he stumbled over it.

Eyes fixed firmly on her face, he willed her to look at him. She did and he was lost in the deep green of her gaze, swimming with tears as her shoulders sagged in relief. She took a step towards him and he didn't hesitate a moment longer. He surged forward, swept her up against his chest and twirled around with her in his arms, unable to control the relief and happiness that drained the blood from his head and charged his veins with a passion that had as much to do with being Greek as it did with being in love. *Oh gods, when had it become love?*

Her face, buried against his neck, was wet with tears. Her arms encircled his neck so tightly he could barely breathe. Still he held her as close as he could, their bodies aligned perfectly, each curve fitting together like a well-cut jigsaw puzzle.

"*S'agapo, omorfi vasilissa mou.*" He untangled her arms from his neck and took her face between his hands. "*Min me afisis pote, agápi mou.*"

The burgeoning crowd around them clapped and giggled. Jax heard nothing except the roar of blood in his ears.

"Yes," whispered Arian.

He smiled, knowing she hadn't understood a word, yet trusting him enough to agree. Closing his eyes against the sweet pain that flooded him, he lowered his head to hers, touched the soft, apple-flavoured lips of temptation with his and drew her into a kiss that had the crowd sighing collectively at the magic and tenderness of it.

Cameras flashed as the media surged forward, a buzz of annoying parasites pulling them apart and dousing the magic with the wave of a microphone boom above them.

"Miss Kendrick … Arian … is this Craig McMahon's competition? Is this the mystery man you dumped the Bachelor of the Year for? Who is he? Where's he from? Did you meet him in Greece or did you know him before you broke up with Craig? Is it true you two-timed Craig McMahon?"

Questions rained on them like hail, cooling their

passion and dragging them back to the stark reality of their surroundings.

"Come." Helen's gentle hand on his arm drew his attention to the television cameras and microphones surrounding them like a shark net. "We are attracting attention. Arian, perhaps we can impose on your hospitality? We will take a taxi to yours, no?"

"No need, I borrowed Dad's SUV. Penny drives it like a pro. We'll be out of here quickly."

Odys stepped forward and ploughed a path through the crowd. "Excuse me. Sorry, no comment. Step aside please. Come on, Penny. Grab Ermioni's bag from Helen, will you? Let's get a move on."

Weaving their way through the questions thrown at them, they followed Odys out of the airport building and into the covered parking area. Leading the way to the car, Penny and Odys argued over who would drive while the rest of the group was silent, except for a few questions from Ermioni which Helen answered quietly in Greek. Jax happily walked hand in hand with Arian, her warm greeting enough for him to know her ex proved little threat. At least, he hoped so. Zeus was not going to be happy about the media attention though, and he expected Helen's phone would ring at any minute.

Glancing over his shoulder, he saw the reporters following them, cameras and microphones ready. Was this Craig McMahon so big a celebrity that Arian's presence to meet their plane had incurred this high an interest? "Let's hurry it up. Are we much further from the car, Penny?"

"Almost there, Jax. We're two rows ahead."

They stepped up the pace, with Penny pressing the remote for the borrowed eight-seater SUV as they got closer. The car unlocked and the rear door rose with quiet ease. Quickly, Odys and Penny tossed the luggage in the back, while the others slipped into their seats and closed their doors on the advancing tide of press and onlookers.

Odys hopped into the driver's seat and Penny handed over the key without protest. "Our place or yours?" she asked.

"At any other time, I'd take that as an invitation, my dearest Penny." Odys grinned. "Whoever's is closest that we can shake off the hounds."

"You wish. Ours then, we're closer than Oakleigh and we have security."

"Yours it is." With a squeal of tyres on concrete, he reversed out of the parking, selected first gear and drove away from the crowd.

Arian's heart beat erratically, torn between the excitement of seeing Jax again and anger at Craig for encouraging the attention of the media. Why couldn't he simply take no for an answer? Thoughts of Craig fled, as Jax squeezed her hand and her heart beat for an entirely different reason. The press of his thigh against hers, the touch of his skin and the casual arm holding her protectively to his side warmed her from head to toe, and she realised how much she'd missed him.

"We have much to discuss, *agape mou.* We will wait until we are out of the public eye. Your Craig has caused much trouble with his interference." Jax's deep, melodic tones washed over her, the velvety sound sending a delicious shiver through her.

"Yes, he has. I'm sorry. I've told him it's over. Craig isn't used to being told no, unfortunately."

A tiny voice in her conscience nagged. What if the media attention put Jax off? What if he decided she wasn't worth the trouble? She looked up at him as he gazed at the passing scenery outside the car window. His beard was a little fuller now, although still neatly trimmed. His hair bleached with gold by the Aegean sun, he looked every inch the god he claimed to be a descendant of. Her fingers itched to trace the leonine line of his jaw, the curve of his cheekbones and the slope of his proud, Grecian nose. His lips twitched and she knew she'd been caught staring. He looked at her, and then leaned down to whisper against her ear.

"Later, my love, when we are alone, you may explore any part of me you like and I shall return the favour." He flashed a heart-stopping smile before kissing her temple gently.

Odys cleared his throat from the front seat. "Hold that thought, Loverboy." He pointed through the windscreen to where the media had already gathered outside Arian and Penny's apartment block, their curiosity peaked by the arrival of their mysterious guests. "We have to get through the frontline first."

Penny laughed. "You make it sound like you're about to fight the Trojan War."

Arian noticed the way Odys' shoulders tensed, even as Jax stiffened beside her.

"You could be closer to the truth than you realise, Miss Penny," said Odys.

CHAPTER NINE

Odys was right, Arian thought as they dodged the media for the third time that day. Thankful the men were built like mining machinery, she ushered Helen and Ermioni ahead of her, with Odys and Penny taking the lead to open the door of the apartment block. It closed behind Jax, bringing up the rear, and cut off the noise from the street with a thump.

The group breathed a unanimous sigh of relief as they waited for the glass elevator to arrive. Arian no longer wanted to think of the chaos on the other side of the glass doors as cameras photographed them through the sparkling clean windows. Where was Melbourne's famous rain when you needed it?

Reaching the sixth floor, they stepped out into the thankfully empty corridor. With a headache pounding behind her eyes, all Arian wanted was a cup of tea. No doubt Penny would crack their last bottle of Chenin Blanc though, and she wouldn't complain.

"Come inside." She waved them over the threshold, closed and locked the door behind them. Tossing her handbag on the hall table, she realised they'd left the luggage in the car.

"No matter," said Odys when she mentioned it. "We can't stay here long. As soon as the ruckus has cleared down there, we'll need to find a way home."

"I'm not sure that will happen tonight." Penny clicked on the television. "We're just in time for the news, and look who's making headlines."

Arian groaned as Channel Twelve's newsreader filled the screen. "Making news tonight … Tornadoes tear through the USA, the Demon Dodgers management team calls an emergency meeting to discuss Craig McMahon's future, and who is the mystery man his ex, Arian Kendrick, picked up at the airport?"

"Picked up? Why do they have to make it sound so darn tacky?" Arian accepted the glass of white from Penny.

Jax stood next to her as they crowded around the television, a comforting hand on her shoulder as the newsreader continued and the image of Arian and Jax's embrace flashed on.

"Demons fans called foul play as Ms Kendrick flew into the arms of a man we can only guess is the lover she ditched Craig McMahon for. The two looked cosy as they dodged the crowd tonight, avoiding questions and escorted by yet another mystery man, a woman and a little girl. Speculation is running high. We'll have more on that tomorrow as new information comes to light."

Taking the remote from Penny, Arian turned off the

television. “Bloody hell, haven’t the bloody media got more important news to report? What a mess.” She looked at the group. “I’m so sorry. This has gotten way out of control.”

“Yes,” Helen agreed. “We saw the newspapers, Arian. This is not your fault.”

Thunder rattled the windows and a flash lit up the sky over Melbourne, bathing it in an eerie glow. Seconds later, rain thrashed down with a vengeance that promised widespread flooding.

“Ah, that should take care of the media camp out,” muttered Odys. “We should take advantage of it and leave now. Jax?”

Jax nodded, and pulled Arian close. “Tomorrow we will talk, I promise.”

“Yes,” she agreed. Slipping her arms around his waist, she hugged him closer and lay her head against his chest to be comforted by the erratic beat of his heart. “Tomorrow.”

He pressed a kiss against her temple, the promise in his touch a comfort to her frayed nerves. “It’s late and we need to get home. Ermioni has had a long day, as have we all. If you could call a taxi for us, my love?”

“Of course.”

Flustered, she unhooked her arms from around him, walked to the hall table and got her phone out of her bag. Three missed calls and four text messages — no doubt all from Craig. The bastard had totally spoiled Jax’s homecoming. Had she really thought he’d give up without a fight? She should have known better.

Just as well they’d come to her apartment. If the press had followed Jax home, they’d hound him mercilessly.

"Arian." She turned to see Jax leaning against the wall, his thumbs hooked through the belt loops of his jeans. "Do you love him, this Craig McMahon?"

Arian looked down at her phone as it rang again and tapped reject. She sighed. "He was so charming, good looking and popular. I was flattered by the attention when I knew he could have his pick of the bunch and he chose me."

Jax pushed away from the wall and stepped closer, making no move to touch her. "And now?"

Warmth radiated from him, tugging her closer. She looked up and in his eyes she saw uncertainty mixed with a touch of sadness, and something that almost resembled desperation. They'd known each other such a short time, yet he'd become as important to her as breathing. Here in the cold reality of Melbourne, could they make a short-lived holiday romance work?

That magic they'd felt on Mykonos, the special connection between them and the glimpses of Paradise when they'd made love — were they all for real?

"No, I don't love him, Jax. I don't think I ever really did, but —"

He cut her words off with a gentle touch of his finger to her lips. "That's all I need to know." His lips replaced the finger on her mouth with a quick tender kiss before he stepped back, leaving her wanting more. "I want to stay with you more than anything, but Odys and I need to see Helen and Ermioni home safely tonight in a taxi. I'll be back tomorrow after a shower and a sleep. We'll talk about our future then, my beautiful *vasilissa*."

Arian wanted to beg him to stay, to hold her for the rest of the night and make her nightmares go away. Deep down though, she knew he was right. It would only get messier if they stayed and tried to leave in the daylight, and they were doing the right thing making sure Helen and Ermioni were safe. God knew what stories the press would make up by tomorrow.

"Okay. Tomorrow. Sure. I'll call for that taxi now." While I still can.

She watched Jax walk back to where Odys and Helen waited in the lounge room, a sleepy Ermioni between them on the couch, torn between begging him to stay and letting him go. The automated booking message played, she gave the address for the pick-up and hung up.

"Your taxi will be here in ten minutes," Arian said, walking into the lounge room. "We'll take you downstairs to get your luggage out of Penny's car." Her words were hollow, like the ache in her heart. She'd pictured their reunion so differently. Now a taxi would sweep him away again at the ungodly hour of two a.m. thanks to bloody Craig McMahon.

"No, you and Penny should stay here. I can't leave you alone in that mob down there. They'll only hound you with questions and turn this into more of a *tragikó théatro*." Jax squeezed her hands. "The luggage can wait for another day. There is nothing in there we need immediately." He turned to the others. "Why don't you guys go ahead and I'll be down in a minute or two?"

Odys cocked an eyebrow. "One minute? That's fast, even for you," he teased, earning himself a punch on the arm from Helen. "What?"

"Behave yourself. Take Ermioni, will you? She's a little heavier these days."

"Yeah, yeah. Hey, Penny — catch." He pulled the car keys out of his pocket and tossed them across to her.

She caught them with ease. "Looks like you need to practise your pitch, big boy. That was too easy."

"Oh, honey, when I put power behind my pitch, you'll know all about it."

"You pitch like a blind man wearing glasses. You're more likely to break a window than a boundary."

He narrowed his eyes at her as he picked Ermioni up into his arms. "Is that a challenge?"

Penny laughed. "Ha, if it was, you couldn't rise to it anyway. I'll walk you to the lift … to make sure you leave."

"You love me, you know you do."

"Like I love a hangover after a night on the town … not."

With a sigh, Helen shepherded the bickering pair out the door, closing it behind them and leaving Jax and Arian alone in the aftermath of deafening silence. Arian's heart beat a tattoo in her chest.

"Arian, we only have a few minutes now so I won't waste time on explanations. There are things I need to tell you and I'm going to need your trust. Tomorrow, I will tell you everything, but I want you to know you mean everything to me and I will fight for you to the end of my days."

A shiver of apprehension spread through her. "Jax —"

"Shh, my love." Gently, he took her face in his hands and lowered his head to whisper against her lips. "I love you, my Faerie Queen. Without you, my soul will die and all I have to live for will be gone for eternity. I cannot let that happen for I do not wish to reside in such hell."

He kissed her then, a soft tender kiss that curled her toes and drained the blood from her head to boil through her veins. A taste of more to come, and a promise of tomorrow as he held her close in the haven of his arms, melting her against him as her temperature rose to fever pitch and she clung to his shirt. A kiss so deep and full of love, Arian felt a tear trickle down her cheek and tasted the salt on his lips.

He lifted his head and held hers gently against his heart for a moment longer. She listened to the unsteady pounding, closing her eyes and absorbing the sound so she'd remember it later.

"Stay," she whispered.

"Tomorrow," he promised, stroking her hair.

Jax cursed the blinding flash of cameras and thrust of microphones as they exited the building. Odys shuffled Helen and Ermioni into the backseat of the waiting taxi, while Jax got into the front seat, and closed the door on the media circus.

"Drive. I'll give you directions when we're away from this mob."

The driver nodded. "Sure thing." With a squeal of tyres, he pulled away from the kerb.

Jax looked back and saw reporters scrambling for their transport to follow. Thankfully, with the taxi driver negotiating a warren of back streets, they lost the horde quickly.

"So, you a celebrity or something?" he asked curiously.

"Or something," Jax replied. "That was smart driving, thank you."

"Where to?"

"Grandview Grove, Oakleigh. You okay back there?" Jax glanced back to see Ermioni sleeping peacefully on Helen's lap. "What a mess. This isn't going to sit well with you-know-who. The media attention is worse than we expected."

Odys sighed. "It will blow over, I'm sure. If we keep a low profile maybe they'll leave us all alone and find someone else to focus on. A few days, a week … that should do it."

A week without seeing or speaking to Arian? He'd go insane, Jax thought. He wasn't about to waste even one day of his godly reprieve.

The look in her eyes had begged him to stay and it had cost him dearly to ignore it. There was nothing he'd like more than to hold her all night long against him, inhale the smell of her perfume and feel the touch of her silky skin on his …

"Cut it out, Jax. I know what you're thinking," Odys groaned. "You'll blow the electrics on the taxi with those thoughts. I don't want to have to walk the last few blocks."

Jax chuckled as they approached the intersection on Estelle Street. Within minutes, they pulled into the driveway of the two-storey home Zeus had acquired for their stay on Earth. The Mediterranean styling and whitewashed walls reminded Jax of home. The only difference was the secret cellar beneath the floor, dug and re-sealed by Zeus' magic to protect the treasure beneath. The Shield of Achilles would finally be his if he succeeded in his mission to marry Arian — Queen of the

Faeries, Restorer of Life — and reclaimed his soul from Purgatory.

Helen carried Ermioni inside while Odys retrieved their luggage from the trunk. Jax handed the driver the fare with a generous tip.

"Thank you. I'd appreciate it if you tell no-one where you dropped us off?"

"Of course, sir." His smile broadened as he counted off the dollar notes in his hand.

"*Kalinýchta.* May the gods be with you." Jax turned and followed Odys up the drive.

They walked hand in hand on the moonlit beach, the waves caressing the shore with a gentle wash, their bodies touching with each step they took on the soft white sand. A warm breeze lifted her hair and blew the strands across her cheek. Arian felt the brush of Jax's fingers against her skin as he tucked the wisps behind her ear. They stopped, feet sinking into the sand as the water lapped at their feet. Jax pulled her close, his head descending and blocking out the light of the full moon as his lips touched hers.

"Arian …" he whispered.

On the horizon, storm clouds built and lightning flashed. Thunder roared as the wind whipped up, sending sand spiralling around them, stinging their legs. A gust ripped Jax from her arms, even as she tried to cling to his waist—

"Arian, wake up. You've got to see this." Penny's voice pierced her dreams and drew her awake.

Arian groaned. "Go away."

Penny shook her firmly. "I mean it, Arian. This is scary shit."

Arian sat up and wiped the remnants of her dream away as Penny turned on the television. The morning show hosts stood on the pavement outside Craig's apartment block, and between them stood the man himself.

"There's a twist in the tale of unrequited love this morning as we go to air live with football's golden boy, Craig McMahon." Amanda Dhiaga preened as she fluttered her false eyelashes at their guest.

"That's right, Amanda," crooned Mal Sebastian. "Who *is* the mystery man Arian Kendrick took home last night? Craig?" He thrust the mike between them.

"That's the question we're all asking, Mal. Arian met this bloke on Paradise Beach in Mykonos. We all know the club there is a pick-up joint where creeps prey on the holidaymakers — spiked drinks, a quick lay and they send them on their way. If they think the mark is worth something, they romance them a little."

"Is that what you think has happened to Arian?" Mal wiggled an eyebrow at the camera.

Arian wished she had magical powers to reach through the screen and slap the sneer from his lips.

"Not think, Mal … I know."

"Oooh," squealed Amanda, scenting scandal. "Do tell."

Craig, the smarmy bastard, placed an arm around Amanda's shoulder, leaned in and said, "I've had him investigated."

"Oh, this is bullshit." Arian made a grab for the remote, intent on turning off the offensive reporting. Penny dodged out of her way.

"I want to hear what crap he's come up with. Then we

can get a hold of Jax and Odys, and they can sue his stupid arse."

Arian threw herself back against her pillows with a huff as Craig leaned forward and delivered his pearl of wisdom.

"Arian's boyfriend, Jax Polemistis, doesn't exist."

The crowd behind them on the pavement gasped, Mal Sebastian sneered and Amanda Dhiaga devoured Craig with her eyes as she inched closer. Arian raised herself on her elbows and looked at Penny, a sick feeling churning in her stomach. Cold dread shivered down her spine.

"That's quite a strong statement there, Craig. He looked pretty real outside her apartment last night." Mal cocked an eyebrow at Craig, who smiled charmingly into the camera.

Arian's skin crawled with goosebumps at the self-assured arrogance in his expression.

"I've had him and his friend investigated … for Arian's protection, you understand."

Arian tossed a cushion at the screen. "For my protection, my arse. You miserable, trouble-making bastard." Even as the words slipped from her lips, she felt the doubt grow like weeds encroaching on her garden of happiness.

"Shh," scolded Penny. "Surely he wouldn't be stupid enough to make a statement like that without any proof."

Arian grumbled as he paused, shoulders straight and a smirk Arian wanted to slap from his lips.

"My investigators found no trace of Ajax Polemistis or Odysseus Laertiades. No business details, no credit information, not so much as a social media account."

Arian felt his arrow hit home as if he stood right in her

bedroom with the bow aimed at her heart. Penny pressed the button on the remote and silence echoed around the room. Silently, she crawled up to sit next to Arian, hugging the spare pillow. For a moment, neither spoke. Too much of what Craig had said made sense. If Jax and Odys were scammers, they were damn good ones. The yacht, Helen and little Ermioni … surely they weren't involved too? And what about those strange mind reading moments, those glimpses of Paradise Arian had seen in his kiss, and the zing of pleasure she'd felt at his touch? They had certainly felt real and there'd been no mistaking Jax's own cries of pleasure.

"That's it, I'm calling Odys," said Penny, launching off the bed and running out the door.

Arian sighed and reached for her phone. With her heart in her throat, she dialled Jax's number. It rang three times.

The number you have called has been disconnected. Please hang up or try again.

Hades chuckled. Humans, they were so predictable and so easy to manipulate. Playing with Craig McMahon's mind was fun even if it wasn't much of a challenge. While McMahon kept the media busy with his whining, it kept the Faerie Queen distracted long enough for Hades to forge a plan. He couldn't have her flitting around with Ajax, becoming friendly with Zeus and finding out about Paradise, could he now?

He swirled his dark cape around his shoulders and hooked in the clasp. His pitch-black stallions snorted and stamped their impatience, and the chariot rocked on its wheels. By the time his dear brother Zeus found out what he was about, Hades would have control of Paradise. He didn't need the Faerie Queen really, but with his wife Persephone away for so many months of the year, she would have come in handy. Never mind, he'd have his fun some other way. *I wonder what Athena's doing these days.*

CHAPTER TEN

Jax and Odys winced as lightning flashed around the room and Zeus paced the tiled floor of their kitchen. "This bloody Earth and their damned technology. Look at the trouble it has caused. Did I not forbid you to engage public attention? Did I not make the rules clear enough before you left Purgatory, Ajax?"

Jax looked at Odys who, by the strangled grin on his face, found their predicament more amusing than frightening. No sooner had they unlocked the front door of the house than Zeus had made his dramatic entrance, swooping down from the sky in his fiery chariot, his harpies' wings spread wide. He'd sworn, ripe and loud, at the bumpy Earth landing, the harpies more used to navigating clouds.

Jax's gaze drifted out the window to the back garden where Helen patched their skinned knees and elbows, and used magic to repair their wings. The chariot hadn't fared well either, although that was more a result of Zeus' fury than the entry through Earth's atmosphere.

"Ajax." Zeus' shout tore Jax's gaze away from the charred remains of the chariot. "Hand me that blasted *tiléfono* thing. You too, Odysseus."

"What? But …" Odys jumped as a lightning bolt struck within millimetres of his big toe. He thrust the mobile phone at Zeus, who held out his free hand to Jax.

"It's my only communication with Arian," pleaded Jax.

"That's the problem with you young people. You've forgotten the art of communication. This —" he wiggled Odys' phone between his fingers, "— is not a means of interaction, it's a curse. Causes accidents, privacy breaches and all sorts of things because humans are lured by its silly magic," he muttered.

The phone disappeared and Odys grumbled, "That curse cost me seven hundred Earth dollars."

"Then you were taken for a fool. Give me that phone, Ajax. Don't make me take it by force."

Jax looked down at the black device and hesitated. Without it, he had no way of contacting Arian. Her apartment was surrounded by reporters thanks to that jerk, Craig McMahon. He couldn't risk going there again, attracting media attention, having them ask awkward questions like why he didn't have a credit card or the business he'd said he owned didn't exist. Now he just looked like every other shady lawyer on the planet. The public sure as hell wasn't ready to hear they'd been invaded by Greek gods.

The phone flew from his hand and into Zeus'. Jax rubbed his palm against his thigh to numb the sting of the fiery separation.

"No reason why you can't communicate the old-fashioned way — by talking face to face. Far more enjoyable, in my opinion." He leaned out the window and yelled, "Helen, I need you in here now. The harpies can fix themselves. They don't need you to pamper them."

"Zeus, keep your voice down or you'll have the whole neighbourhood awake. Imagine the chaos that will create." Helen flapped her hands at him.

"Bah, I stopped time. The earthlings won't have any memory of tonight's blasted spectacle. We have work to do before morning." He pulled back inside, walked to the chair and plopped down onto it, rubbing his soot-blackened knees. "You two will be the death of me, I swear."

"The harpies are settled in the garage for the night," said Helen, closing the back door behind her. "They've promised to behave and stay there until further instructions. I'll need to take in some food and blankets before sunrise —" She looked at her watch, "— in about an hour. What's the plan, Zeus?"

"The media and that damn footballer are the last of our worries right now. I've had a message from the water faeries on Paradise. The word in the realms is that Hades is making his way there on a takeover bid. We need to get Arian there now."

Arian shivered against the early morning chill as she stood on her apartment balcony and watched the sun rise. What was Jax doing now? Neither she nor Penny had felt much like sleeping last night. Too many unanswered questions had twirled around in their heads so instead they'd trawled the internet for information on either Jax or Odys, and come up with nothing. Craig was right — not a mention of them anywhere. Her mind fought a battle with her heart. Surely a man who'd made love with the passion and commitment Jax had, said the things he did with such conviction, and showed her a glimpse of Paradise in a simple kiss — surely he couldn't be the rat bastard Craig was making him out to be?

Puffy clouds blotted the horizon in an angry shade of red as the sun did its best to rise above them. In the distance, a helicopter buzzed low like a dragonfly on a pond.

"Red sky in the morning, shepherd's warning ..." Penny pushed a warm mug of coffee into Arian's cold hands.

She took it gratefully and wrapped her fingers around it, welcoming the warmth that seeped through her at her first sip. "I wonder what's going on over there. That helicopter is flying awfully close to the ground."

"News chopper," said Penny. "Oakleigh had a bad storm last night. Freak winds tore off roofs and spot fires started from lightning strikes."

Arian frowned. "That doesn't make sense. We had nothing here."

Penny shrugged. "The weather has been very unpredictable lately. Remember that waterspout in Western Australia a couple of months back? The tornado that caused that cleaned up a construction site. They're still trying to fix that mess."

"Oakleigh — that's where Jax and Odys live ..." A memory teased Arian's mind.

"Yep. Storms seem to follow them wherever they go, don't they? Thing is, I checked the Bureau of Meteorology site, and other than a few standard rainclouds, the bureau had no storm warnings in place. Weird." Penny sipped her coffee.

Storms seem to follow them … Arian shrugged off the feeling of unease that tripped at her nerve endings. *I'm being silly.* The weather bureau in Mykonos had explained the storms Arian and Penny had seen there as an unseasonal pocket of humidity.

"On the upside, the media vans have cleared out. I'm not sure Craig will be happy about being upstaged by a freak storm." Penny peered over the edge of the balcony rail.

Arian smiled. No, Craig wouldn't be happy at all. "Do you think they're really scammers?"

"Jax and Odys?" Penny shrugged. "I never got that vibe from them, but then we haven't been very good at judging the difference, have we? Look at Simon and Craig. I never would have picked them as dickheads and look how they turned out."

Arian drained the coffee from the mug and took a moment to answer. "A volatile mix of ego and fame. I wish we could find something — some sort of evidence — that would prove Craig wrong."

"I hear ya. Just because they're not on Google, doesn't mean they don't exist. They might prefer to keep a low profile on what it is they do. Who knows what cases Jax defends that might put him or his clients in danger and, well, nightclubs attract some dangerous people too, so you can't blame Odys for wanting to keep a low profile, I guess."

Arian shook her head. “I’m going to shower. It might clear my head.” She handed Penny her empty mug. “I can’t shake the feeling that there is something … unusual … about them. Not in a bad way. Just too many secrets between them.” Or perhaps it was Craig getting to her, casting doubts in her mind as he tried to sway things in his favour.

“You’re right, and I’m sure there’s a good explanation for it. We just haven’t found it yet, and *I* sure as hell am not ready to give up on them. Not until we have some answers.”

Arian pulled her jumper around her as she shivered against the cold. “I shouldn’t let Craig mess with my mind, but I can’t help wondering … If Jax shows up before I’m finished in the shower, it’s okay to send him in.”

“Right,” said Penny, drawing out the vowels. “What makes you think he’ll show up early?”

“He’ll want to get here before the media does.”

“Damn, here I was thinking you’d turned psychic on me.” Penny grinned. “I wonder if Odys will come too.”

Arian shook her head and smiled. “I thought you didn’t care what Odys does? I think you might like him more than you’re willing to admit.“

With a pat on Penny’s shoulder, she stepped inside and walked to her room, her mind filled with thoughts clamouring for attention. The more she tried to sort through the noise in her head, the more muddled the situation became and the fewer logical answers formed. Arian collected her clothes — jeans, a t-shirt and clean undies—and headed for the bathroom, banishing all thoughts to a corner of her mind. She’d dwell on it later.

Turning on the hot water, she undressed as she waited

until the steam rose before mixing it with cold. She slipped in under the warm spray, and enjoyed the sluice of water that eased over her body, relaxing muscles and washing away the tension that had seized her back and shoulders.

There had to be a reasonable explanation for everything that had happened, both in Mykonos and here. Penny would Google until her fingers were numb to get to the bottom of it, because that's what her friend did best. Craig was obviously in it for no-one other than himself. How had she been so blind to his ego until now?

She closed her eyes and tipped her head back, letting the water flow over her hair, wetting it to a darker shade of red. Arian reached for the shampoo, her eyes flying open as her hand came in contact with a warm masculine one she knew well.

"Jax." Her heartbeat sped up at the touch of his skin against hers.

Jax grinned. "You knew I was coming."

"Yes, but I'm not sure how I knew." She'd felt his need to reach her as she'd stood on the balcony watching the sun rise over Oakleigh, a desperation too uncanny to explore or explain.

"You will understand soon, *agape mou*." His mouth turned serious as he nibbled his lip. "I had to see you, Arian. We need to talk."

She felt the caress of his eyes over her body, which tightened in response. "Now?"

"Your thoughts are driving me crazy. I can hear them tumbling around as you seek answers, but the truth needs to come from me."

"You've seen the news?"

He nodded. "McMahon is wrong, Arian. We are not

scammers or scoundrels. He might not have found the information he was looking for, but I promise you every moment of our history is recorded if one knows where to look."

"That's what Penny said. Well, something like that anyway."

He looked at her through the gap in the shower curtain he'd pulled aside, and held her gaze with his. "Remember on Mykonos I said there were things I couldn't tell you until you trusted me?"

Arian nodded. Mykonos — where life had been a whole lot simpler.

"Do you trust me yet, *agape mou?*" His gaze searched hers, begging her to look beyond Craig's mind games and at what lay between them.

"I don't know. I'm so confused ..." She looked away.

"Will you let me hold you a little? I need the courage of your touch."

Sensibility warred with the need that echoed in her heart. Perhaps both of them needed courage to hear the truth, to look beyond the impossible, and believe the unbelievable.

"I want to trust you." The man who stood before her epitomised everything she'd dreamed of — sexy, kind, and a caring lover. His eyes shone with humour while his body promised strength and protection.

"Then look inside my heart when I hold you." His hands gripped the bottom of his t-shirt. "May I?"

Arian watched as he pulled it up and over his head, exposing his golden chest with its light dusting of dark hair to her gaze. "Yes," she whispered, taking a moment to appreciate the view. No matter what lay between them, what trouble kept them apart, what she needed most right now was to feel the solid reality of his flesh against hers, the reassurance of his hands on her skin, and the sweet taste of his lips on hers.

Her heart changed pace, slowing to a steady rhythm of expectation as he unsnapped the button on his jeans, slid the zipper down at an agonisingly slow pace and worked the denim down strong, muscular legs. Need, liquid and prickly, flowed between her own as she took in every gorgeous inch of his body.

He stepped into the cubicle, shampoo in one hand and drawing her against him with the other. "Good morning, my Faerie Queen."

"We should talk first ..."

"Later. I have a lot to explain and I'll need you to trust me. First though, I need to hold you."

Arian had no intention of arguing. She felt what he did. The urgency for reassurance that what lay between them was real, that what they felt for each other deserved a chance. Reaching up, she cupped his cheeks, the brush of his beard against her palms heightening the pleasure that rushed through her.

"Good morning." She returned the smile that spread across his mouth and met him halfway to touch her lips to his in a too brief, sweet kiss.

His gaze never leaving hers, he reached behind her to tip shampoo into his palm. Placing the bottle on the shelf, he began a slow, sensual massage of her scalp as he worked the subtly scented liquid through her hair.

Arian relaxed against him as sensations spiralled through her. Lust pooled like hot lava between her thighs with each touch of his fingertips, leaving her weak and wanting. She stroked her hand across his abdomen, pleased when a growl rumbled in his chest and his erection grew harder between them. As his hands smoothed the length of her hair down her back, she angled her hips and arched her back, baring her breasts for the attention she craved.

Jax held her hips to him, stroking her skin with one hand while the other teased her nipples to tight rosebuds, sensitive under the smooth caress of his fingertips. She arched back further, tipping back her head and letting the water stream the shampoo from her hair. Jax adjusted his hold so the smooth tip of his erection teased the sensitive nub at her entrance. Arian bit back a sigh of pleasure and squirmed against him, clutching at the rock hard forearms that supported her weight. She pulled herself up against him and raised her face for his kiss.

"I am alive when I am with you," he whispered against her lips as he lifted her into his arms.

"Make love to me, Jax. Make me yours." Arian wrapped her arms around his shoulders and stroked a path down his back. She pressed her mouth to his, tracing her tongue across his lips until he opened them and devoured her with a kiss that sent shockwaves plummeting to her core.

Desperate to connect, to feel the silky length of him making her his own, she clasped her legs tightly around his hips, slipped her hand between them and brought him home. Spreading his legs to take her weight, he leaned back against the cool tiles and Arian welcomed the sensation as he inched deeper inside her. No longer able to control her white-hot desire for him, she clenched her muscles around him and rode, pleased when she drove him to tear his mouth from hers and cry out words in his mother tongue that left no doubt as to his own state of yearning.

She felt him swell and plunge, took what he offered and more. Lips against his neck, she teased the corded muscles with her tongue, nipped at the lobe of his ear and sucked at the sensitive spot below it.

"Arian!" The cry ripped from his throat and pulsed against her lips as he surged into her, his fingers gripping the soft swell of her bottom.

She rode harder until she could no longer hold off the orgasm that rose steadily to meet his. Together they came, hard and fast, almost desperate. As he shuddered against her, spilling his life blood inside her, their lips met in a promise of commitment — to what, they'd have to find out later. All that mattered right now was that they had each other … again and again, as if too soon what they shared would be torn away from them by the storm that raged outside the window.

CHAPTER ELEVEN

The girls and their gods sat around the table, sipping wine and nibbling on the baklava Odys and Jax had brought with them, a present from Helen and Ermioni. Jax sat close to Arian, her hand in his, afraid to let go in case she disappeared, terrified she'd kick him out — dump him — when she heard what he had to say. Would she believe him?

Arian squeezed his hand encouragingly. Still he hesitated. With her by his side, his heart could beat forever, but if she left him his days were numbered, and Hades waited in the wings with his chariot of death ready to transport him to an eternity in hell.

"Should I go first, Jax? Pave the way for your story? I don't have as much to lose as you do … yet." Odys looked at Penny, who glowered at him across the table.

Jax wondered if they'd had a fight while he and Arian were closeted behind her bedroom door to take advantage of every moment of happiness they had together. He shook his head.

"No, it needs to be told and I'll do it." He raised Arian's hand to his lips and pressed a kiss against her fingertips. "Please, trust me, *agape mou*?"

He saw the flicker of confusion in her eyes and prayed he'd done enough to convince her that what he was about to say was nothing but the truth. He took a sip of wine, squeezed her hand, and stood. Restless, he walked to the window and looked out at the rain falling softly beyond the glass. The dark storm clouds had lightened to a dull, damp grey, and the helicopters over Oakleigh had gone. Clearly Zeus had things under control again. If only Jax had.

Jax turned and leaned against the windowsill. Crossing his arms, he began. "Remember in the cove in Mykonos, the day we took you sailing? We told you we were descendants of the gods Odysseus and Ajax. We lied."

"What?" Penny sent Odys a black look.

"Well, not lied exactly … perhaps we bent the truth a little. Be quiet and listen, Penny." Odys topped up her wine glass.

"We are ..." Jax paused and ran a hand through his hair. He braced himself and looked Arian in the eyes. He wanted her to see the truth there, wanted most of all for her to believe him. "I am Ajax the Great. I fought the Trojan War and laid claim to the Shield of Achilles."

Arian looked away to study her hands clasped tightly on the table. He'd seen her complexion pale and tears glitter in her eyes before she'd dropped her gaze from his.

"No, it can't be true. Don't do this, Jax. Please, don't lie to me," she whispered, the ache in her voice heartbreakingly clear to his ears.

"Arian, please, *agape mou ...*" If he lost her now — he moved towards her, knelt next to her chair, covered her cold hands with his and begged. “Hear me out before you pass judgement on me? Zeus has granted me a reprieve. I’ve been given the opportunity to redeem my honour, to right my wrongs and earn back my soul.”

Arian kept her eyes fixed on her hands, the knuckles white with tension. Jax placed his forefinger under her chin and tipped it so she raised her eyes to his, shimmering pools of green. He stroked a stray tear from her cheek.

“I swear on Zeus’ honour, I am telling you the truth, my lady Arian. Athena set me up for the fall from grace. She wanted Odysseus to have the Shield of Achilles because she claimed to be in love with him. First she set Odysseus and me against each other, driving a wedge in our friendship, and then she dishonoured me with drug-induced hallucinations that led to the slaughter of the sheep.” Jax took Arian’s clenched hands in his and kissed the tensed knuckles, before laying his forehead on the back of her hands.

“I had no choice but to fall on my sword, to take my own life, rather than face the wrath of Zeus, for I did not deserve the honour of the Shield of Achilles. Odysseus won it fair and square.”

Arian sat as still as death beside his bowed head. Only her hands trembled against his forehead. His throat ached with the need to beg her forgiveness, her understanding … her trust. Silence echoed between the walls of the apartment, while outside the world seemed to hold its breath. No rain against the windows, no thunder from the skies … only deathly silence.

Jax closed his eyes and waited for the final blow to fall as Arian withdrew her hands. He kept his head down, his heart aching as he relived the humiliation of his demise, knowing he'd do it again if he lost her. A gentle hand stroked his hair and hope flared once more. He moved ever so slightly and placed his head on her lap, where she continued to soothe him, saying nothing. He heard the thoughts tumbling over in her mind. The ache in her heart echoed his as she seesawed between disbelief and the need to trust him, to give him a chance.

He ignored Zeus' instructions not to read her mind. If his punishment for that was death, so be it. This was no longer a battle for his soul, for without Arian there was no reason to live. When had it come to that? She was so much more than the one who could rescue him from eternity at Hades' feet, so he listened to the turmoil and prayed.

Minutes ticked by until Penny broke the silence. "*Phwoar.* That's … jeez … I'm not sure I know *what* it is. Radical? Messed up? I think we need a drink. This confession calls for something stronger than a Semillon." She stood, retrieved her prized bottle of ouzo from the top shelf of the pantry and poured a hefty shot into four clean wine glasses.

Odys cleared his throat, took a slug of ouzo and said, "Zeus would like an audience with both of you, Arian and Penny. We are to take you to the house in Oakleigh, if you are willing to come."

Arian raised her head to meet Odys' pleading look, and Jax's heart skipped a beat as he heard the conclusion of her thoughts. She hooked a finger under Jax's chin and forced him to look at her. "I want to trust you, to believe this is real — with all my heart — but how do I know the truth? How do I know for sure you're not the crazy con artist Craig thinks you are? What sane man tells a twenty-first century woman he's a real Greek god when even the myths are not proven to be anything more than the drunken ramblings of ancient storytellers? I've been taken for a fool before, Jax. I never want to be taken for one again."

"You are no fool, my love, only unawakened to who you really are, who I am, and what wonders lie beyond Earth's boundaries. Come with me, *agape mou*. Let me show you the truth. Trust me, one more time."

Penny eyed the twin monsters as they hovered above the balcony later that night. "Holy crappy noodles, what the hell are those? Birds? People?"

"Harpies — spirits of the wind — also known as the hounds of Zeus. The myths painted them as thieving beings dispatched by the gods to snatch away people and things from the earth." Odys lowered his voice as he said the words, and chuckled when Penny shivered. "Don't worry, Penny, they're simply our means of transportation today so we don't get hounded by the press at street level."

"I hope to God you're right because if kidnap is on the agenda, you'd better be prepared for a fight. They look a little worse for the wear. Can they manage our weight?"

Odys grinned. "The journey to Earth took its toll, hence the missing feathers, but they're tougher than they look."

"They're so soft. I expected them to look a little more … Greek?" Penny rubbed a patch of feathers where they glittered in the moonlight on the closest harpy's side.

"Ah, yes. They're going through a manga phase at the moment … teenagers, you know. They've watched a little too much Earth television and become hooked on *Sailor*

Moon. Come on, hop on." He called the harpy closer and helped Penny onto its back. "Hold on tight, like you're going for a piggy back ride."

"I'm not sure your manga harpy would appreciate the reference to a cartoon animal. How safe is this thing anyway?" Penny squealed loudly as the harpy dipped suddenly. It went into a spiral dive, before swooping back up with Penny clinging to its neck, her face buried against the harpy's shoulder and her legs clenched around its waist.

"Behave, Aello," Odys ordered. "Safer than driving in Melbourne and dodging the trams. Don't worry, I'll be right beside you on Celaeno. I won't let you fall far."

"Very bloody funny, Odys. You're such a charming hero." Penny squealed again as the harpies took off into the dark, moonlight breaking through the clouds to glisten on their wings.

Arian smiled up at Jax and gripped his arm with both hands. "This is surreal. I keep pinching myself to see if I'm awake. I'm off to meet *Zeus*." She stilled and cuddled closer for a moment. "What if Craig finds out about this? He'll ridicule you publicly, make the press think you're insane." For a moment, panic seized her and she stiffened at his side. If the papers got hold of the story, they'd have a field day with the impossible truth, make fun of them all.

Jax hugged her and kissed her temple. "Zeus has taken precautions by opening a small portal for us to travel through."

Arian nodded and raised her face to the skies as Jax whistled. Of course he had. He'd probably waived his aegis and sent the unsuspecting world to sleep so the harpies could steal away women who would be reported as missing persons the next day.

"The real world carries on below us, none the wiser. Are you ready?"

"I'm not sure about this ..." Once again, apprehension flowed through her, until she caught sight of the bird-woman sailing the air currents as gracefully as a swan.

The harpy that swooped down was larger, older and very definitely proud mythical Greek. Dark brown feathered wings were highlighted by gold streaks that caught the moon's rays. Her naked body was coated in shades of gold and cinnamon. She bowed before Jax and then spread her wings wide, angling towards the balcony much like a ship docks against the wharf.

"This is Electra, the twins' mother." Jax helped Arian onto her back and slipped on behind her, holding her tightly against him as he picked up the reigns. "Go gently, wise Electra. It is my queen's first time."

The harpy dipped her head and flew towards Oakleigh, riding the air currents gracefully with gentle turns and low swoops. The wind rushed through Arian's hair, and she raised her face to it … freedom. The cobwebs of uncertainty fled as she looked around her. In the distance, lightning flashed from gathering storm clouds edged with silver, and the moon's rays danced with the stars — an impossible picture painted on the canvas of the night sky.

Arian looked down. The landscape was bathed in shadows. She caught glimpses of movement below, head and tail lights on the Monash Freeway, the gas brigade outside the Crown Casino spouting flames skywards and lighting up the Yarra River. Years of flying across the land in the Cessna could not compare with Melbourne's magic at night from the saddle of a mythical bird.

"Tell me I'm not dreaming, Jax," she whispered.

His arms tightened around her, the reins he held loosely in his hands resting against her thighs. "It's real, Arian. Can you feel the magic? You have it in you, my lovely. All it needs is awakening."

She pressed back into his chest, the strength of it offering reassurance, and closed her eyes. The wind whistled past her ears and in it she heard laughter, light and happy, tinkles and giggles that made her think of fairies. Jax's fingers entwined with hers and squeezed gently, as his face touched hers, cheek to cheek. His thoughts nudged hers towards Paradise where he showed her a Faerie Queen, dressed in flowing silk robes of aqua, a crown of wildflowers in her hair.

"That's you, my Queen of the Faeries, in your queendom in Paradise. That's who you really are."

Questions tumbled through her mind, things she should ask, visions she should deny, but up here above the hustle and bustle of Melbourne there was only magic and a peace she wanted to enjoy for as long as it lasted.

Almost too soon, they landed gently in the garden in Oakleigh, while around them the suburb slept, cloaked by magic and the night. Penny hooked her arm through Arian's as soon as they were off the harpies' backs and on the ground. "Oh. My. God. I could get used to that. Like riding a Harley, only better."

Odys snorted. "You haven't ridden a Harley with me yet. Let me know when you've plucked up the courage and I'll show you how it's done," he said.

Penny ignored him and walked towards the house, taking Arian along with her. "Are you scared?"

"Petrified. If this is really happening, we're about to meet Zeus, god of all gods," Arian answered.

"I Googled him, but all the pictures of the statues are so damn ugly. I can't believe he's that gross, not when Jax, Odys and Helen are so damn beautiful."

Arian didn't respond, still wrapped up in the wonder of the flight, Jax's warmth on her back and the vision she'd seen of herself. All this, so far removed from reality. She'd pinched herself to make sure she was awake as soon as Jax had helped her down off the harpy. She rubbed the reddened skin. Craig's words taunted her, drugs, con artists. Had they slipped LSD into the wine? Tainted the baklava with marijuana or some other hallucinogen? What had they to gain by drugging and abducting them, though? And why do it in such a magical way? If they meant her and Penny any harm, surely tying them up, knocking them out and dumping them in a white panel van would have been a much quicker and more acceptable way.

"I read that Zeus can produce storms and intense darkness by simply shaking his aegis. Thunder rolls, lightning flashes, and clouds pour rain at his command. Maybe that explains all the weird storms we've been having lately." Penny sighed.

Arian stopped walking and clutched Penny's arm. She looked back to see Odys and Jax leading the harpies towards the garage. "Myths also tell of how the gods drugged and abducted women, and kept them as virtual slaves."

Penny pulled her into a hug. "Think about it, love. If they wanted to hurt us, they had loads of opportunity to do it on Paradise Beach where no-one knew who we were. They wouldn't have waited until we got home to do it. Besides, I see how Jax looks at you, Arian, and there's no doubt in my mind he's fallen faster and harder than Troy for you." She held Arian away and dropped her hands to her side. "I wish Odys looked at me the way Jax looks at you. Instead, he thinks I'm a pain in the arse." Penny smiled as if that thought gave her more pleasure than any romantic attention ever could.

Arian laughed. "I can't believe you're taking all this in your stride. I'm convinced I'm having hallucinations. This is surreal. It's so wrong yet in my heart I know it's right. Have I lost my mind, Penny? Is this a dream I'm going to wake up from?"

Penny shrugged. "If it is, then I'm crazy too. I mean … what on earth does Zeus want from me? You were raised on Welsh folklore and there was definitely something special about your gran, so there's a chance that there's a little magic in you … but me? I'm definitely all mortal. The only magic I know is how to make balloon animals to hand out at kids' birthday parties."

Arian laughed. "Yes, but ..." She dropped her voice to a whisper. "You're in love with Odys. That makes you Zeus' business."

Penny froze. "I *so* am not."

"Not what?" Odys almost ran her over as he and Jax caught up with them. She looked at him, mouth agape with words that wouldn't come, so he patted her on the bum and said, "Move on. We can't keep the boss waiting."

Jax caught up with Arian as she walked on, leaving Penny to work it out.

"Everything okay?"

She nodded and slipped an arm around his waist. “Perfect.”

The back door opened and Helen waited to receive them on the threshold. “Welcome, Arian, Penny. Come, I have tea ready. Zeus has indulged a little too much in his brew, I’m afraid. Anyone would think he is nervous about this meeting.”

“I can hear you, Helen.” Zeus’ deep voice reached for them from the depths of the house.

Helen ignored him and winked. “He’s discovered Twitter.”

Jax and Odys groaned.

“Please tell me you’re monitoring his tweets?”

“What’s he tweeting?”

She looked at her friends and grinned. “First let’s take care of business. Come.”

Helen led the way through the kitchen into the lounge room where Zeus sat feet up, leaning back in a recliner.

“I’m tweeting up a storm,” he said. “Ermioni showed me how.”

“Ermioni did? Isn’t she a little young for that?” Odys frowned.

“Only in Earth years.”

“What have you tweeted about?” Jax wasn’t sure he wanted to know the answer.

“About the game on Saturday. How *you* are going to kick some Demon Dodgers’ arse. Ah, the girls are here. Come here, let me look at you.” He pushed the footrest of the recliner back in and tilted the chair into the upright position. “There are some Earth things I do like and this chair is definitely going home to Olympus.” He studied Penny first. “Mmm … yep, perfect.”

His gaze slid to Arian and she squirmed a little under it. His eyes bored into her soul, leaving her exhausted mentally and physically as he rummaged around in her memories and brought the important ones to the fore.

"Your grandmother would be proud of you, girl. You've done well at keeping her secret. I met her a few times in the magic realm. Quite an exotic beauty she was. Sadly more mortal than she deserved, it appears, since she has gone from this world."

"What secret?" Arian's thoughts whirled. Gran hadn't told her anything she didn't share with others, nor had she said anything about keeping secrets. How could this man possibly have met her gran? In the magic realm?

Even as the thoughts formed, she remembered the nights after Gran had put her to bed as a child when she'd creep out to watch as Gran took down the big leather-bound book from the shelf and wrote in it. She'd light a candle and whisper in Welsh. When she'd asked Gran about it, she'd said she was saying her prayers, and then she'd taught Arian the words that had scared off the monster in the sea on Paradise Beach.

How could she have forgotten about that? Those fierce red eyes, the smell of sulphur and the scream of pain before the thing had disappeared, the fear and evil she'd felt in its presence ... could it be that all those stories Gran had told about dragons, fairies and beasties were true? That she really had lived in another world, apart from the one she'd retreated to when Alzheimer's had struck?

"Ahh, my child. Your gran never had Alzheimer's at all. That's a little trick we use to wipe memories so the soul can be reincarnated. Sometimes we leave a little behind and call it deja vu, so the soul can recognise its humble beginnings." He leaned forward and patted her hand. "Now, you may call me Zeus. No need to stand on ceremony down here. I bid you welcome, your highness." He eased out of his chair, stood and bowed to her.

Her curtsey came as a surprise to her, the movement natural and graceful as if she was born to do it.

"Thank you … Zeus." Arian clasped her hands in front of her as she straightened, grateful for the steadying comfort of Jax's hand under her elbow. Zeus' presence alone packed an energy-draining punch, never mind that he'd foraged in her deepest memories. *Believe the unbelievable,* Gran's words echoed in her mind. Every story Gran had ever told her, she'd ended with those words.

He nodded. "Sit, my children. We have much to plan and discuss. Helen, we'll take that tea now, thank you. I need a clear head. The Earth's atmosphere has me a little light-headed."

"Of course, it has nothing to do with the two goblets of brew you threw back while you waited for Jax and Odys to return, does it?" Helen teased.

"I might have added a few extra fermented grapes," Zeus confessed. "Arian, come and sit here with me, child. You too, Penny … on the other side." He waved at the two armchairs next to him, set at an angle. "Now, Arian, I have a little gift for you." He reached over and lifted a heavy tome from the table beside him. "Do you recognise this, my dear?"

"Gran's book." She took it from him as he handed it over, clutching it to her chest and breathing in the comforting smell of Gran and old leather. "How did you get this? I searched for it everywhere when I packed up the house after Gran died. I couldn't find it."

Tears stung her eyes. She'd thought perhaps it was a diary she could read, a link she'd have to the stories of Gran's past, but when she searched for it amongst the things she'd kept, it was gone.

"Arianrhod gave it to me for safekeeping when I visited her in the respite home just before she passed over. She asked me to safeguard it for you until you were ready. Of course, she forgot to tell me you didn't know the truth."

Arian lowered the book to her lap and stroked the flat of her palm over the smooth cover. Warmth spread up through her hand and enveloped her like one of Gran's big warm hugs. She caught the scent of lavender and jasmine in the air as peace flowed through her body and into her heart. "The truth about what?"

"Do you believe in magic, Arian?"

She shrugged. Fairytales were one thing, but when they came to life they tended to be a little confronting. Harpies, Greek gods, Zeus … they surrounded her … in the flesh. Balanced on her knees was a book that vibrated with power and spread warmth and peace through her. "I work with facts, the sciences of land survey. I know about precious metals and conductors, and the solid, touchable matter that makes up our soil here on Earth." She opened the heavy cover of the book to cast her eye over Gran's elegant, flowy, old-fashioned writing, caught sight of an ancient map and sketches of beautiful beings. "This could just be a story book and what I'm feeling mere emotion."

Zeus smiled, leaned over and placed his hand on hers. "Between those pages lies the truth of your existence, your inheritance and your future. It's a lot to take in. We're here to help you, to guide you. The bottom line, my dear, is that you are the Queen of Paradise — a faerie queendom just outside Earth's realm — and your people are under threat from Hades."

Hearing it said didn't make it true, she thought as her logical mind warred against acceptance. Yet deep in her heart she knew … she'd always known … there was something different about her life, some greater force she carried with her and had never understood. If this was all true and not some drug-induced hallucination, somewhere out there was a world where she truly belonged and people who needed her. How could she fight an enemy she couldn't see or didn't believe in?

"Take your time, my dear Arian. Your acceptance will come. Tonight, sleep with the book under your pillow and you will know the truth by morning. Now, I want to hear all about your first harpy flight before we get some sleep. Tomorrow, it's down to business."

Sleep was the last thing on their minds as Arian lay snuggled into Jax's side, head on his chest, his heartbeat steady in her ear. She should be exhausted, frightened, wondering when the downer would come. Instead the only drug in her system was Jax and the sense of coming home.

Her dreams were filled with visions of a castle, beautiful faeries in colourful, flowing silk, handsome guards in livery of royal purple and gold, and Gran telling her to believe in the unbelievable. By morning, as Zeus had promised, she was almost ready to believe.

Now, with the sun streaming in the kitchen window of

the house in Oakleigh, they sat eating breakfast with the great god Zeus while harpies slept in the garage.

She looked at Zeus across the table and he winked back at her. "Sleep well, my dear? I had to put a spell of silence on that damn house alarm to stop it going off."

Arian blushed. *Cheeky bugger*.

"Zeus," Helen scolded at his side.

Zeus chuckled. "What? Love is a thing to be enjoyed, is it not? Your television people even made a series out of it. Captain Stubing on the *Loveboat*. I'm a bit like him, aren't I? Steering people together?"

Arian's lips twitched. If he wasn't such a philanderer she might be a little in love with him herself. His sense of humour was hard to resist. How many women had fallen prey to that cheeky grin?

"Ask, my dear. No need to think it. I have nothing to hide. Ask away."

Arian lay her spoon in her cereal bowl and thought a moment longer. Now it was Zeus' turn to blush. A soft smile curved his lips and crinkled his eyes.

"Now who's being cheeky? Yes, the rumours are true. I have loved many women. Your grandmother was one I admired and loved in a different way, though. She was beautiful, ethereal, and oh so stately at home in Paradise — a woman far above a man like me."

Arian took a sip of her coffee. Greek, rich, strong and thick. "How so when you're the god of gods?"

He chuckled, the sound naughty and husky. No wonder women — both mortal and nymph — had fallen at his feet. If he shed a few years ...

Jax's arm came around her shoulders and he tugged her

closer, pressing a kiss to her temple. "He'd still be old enough to be your father," he whispered in her ear.

Arian laughed and squeezed his hand where it rested on her collarbone. "Come on, Zeus, why was Gran so special to you?"

Zeus pushed away the plate of fruit he'd nibbled on and leaned forward, elbows on the table. "Not just to me, my dear. To everyone she met. She loved your grandfather with all her heart, leaving no room for another. Not even when he died. She fought Hades for his soul and lost. Her sacrifice was mortality."

"Are you saying ...?" Arian's breath hitched in her throat. Gran had said Grandad had died in battle. She'd assumed it was during one of the World Wars.

"World War I was a cover up. It wasn't the world at war, it was the universe. Hades and I both wanted Earth more than anything else. It was the closest to Paradise I could get. For Hades, it was a playground of destruction. It still is … which is why he tried a second time and will keep on trying."

"Grandad?"

"He was on my side but Hades got to him first, at the Battle of Gallipoli. His injuries should not have been life threatening." Zeus shifted in his seat, the haunted look on his face proof he relived the battle. "Hades made a bargain with Arianrhod that day. If she left with him, your grandfather could live. If she stayed, he'd die. She drove a hard bargain before I got there. I was too late. She sold her soul to the devil and he didn't have the guts to keep the bargain. Your grandfather died on the way to the field hospital and your grandmother sacrificed her soul for nothing. I did the best I could to slow the ageing process for her, to keep her alive as long as I could so she could raise you, Arian. Hades collected before she could tell you the truth about the queendom and who you really are."

An almost tangible silence fell around the table until Odys shattered it. "We need to get ready, Zeus. The media interview is booked for 11:30 a.m. outside Jax's newly acquired offices at the courthouse."

"*Efcharisto,* Odysseus." Across the table he took Arian's hand in his. "This is my chance to pay your grandmother back, Arian. To make things right, to give you the piece of Paradise that should have been hers, and to present you with the gift of immortality so you may share it with the man who deserves a soul. Jax is a warrior and a good man, and if he is as clever as I think he is, he will make the right choices when it comes time for the war. Craig McMahon is a small battle that must be fought to silence his need for the limelight, and to stop him bringing attention on us. The real war sits with Hades."

"Too friggin' late," muttered Jax. "You can't stop the McMahon media circus." For the first time since the Battle of Troy, Jax felt the savage need to drive a sword through his enemy and end the whole fiasco.

Zeus narrowed his eyes. "Murder won't save you from Purgatory, Ajax the Great. You need to prove yourself a chieftain worthy of your opponent in order to claim your peace."

"They do things differently here, Zeus. Calling McMahon out to battle would raise a few suspicions, don't you think?"

"Your cockiness will be your downfall, my boy. One doesn't always have to declare war with guns. There are other ways to fight a battle. Hear me out," said Zeus after a long sip of coffee, and sighed. "Football."

Jax looked at Odys who shrugged and shook his head.

"Football," repeated Zeus. "The Demon Dodgers have a charity football match coming up. You should play. Football is a bloodless battle of skill — well, as bloodless as any contact sport can be. It requires tactics and teamwork —" he cocked an eyebrow at Odys, "— and tricky manoeuvres. The object of the game of football is to drive the ball into the opposing team's goal in order to score points, just as our friend — I use the term lightly — Craig McMahon has done with his infernal fire-stoking with the media. It's time to play Mr Australian Football Superstar at his own game. We Greeks invented the bloody game after all. The two of you are bigger football stars on Olympus than that little possum is here on Earth. Win the game and he'll go into hiding to lick his wounds. A blow to his ego is all he needs."

"Football ..." Jax shook his head. He'd much rather Zeus strike the obnoxious bastard with a lightning bolt and send him to hell with Hades. "I don't see how that will fix our situation."

"You will if you listen to me for a change." The angry boom of Zeus' voice echoed through the kitchen.

"Hush, you'll wake Ermioni," scolded Helen.

"That child sleeps like the dead, so don't hush me. Tomorrow I will make a statement to the press to defend these childish claims the troublesome football player is making." He topped up his mug. "Tonight, Helen will work her magic with these machines they call computers and create the records we need to prove your identities."

"In some worlds that's called fraud," chipped in Odys. He flinched as anger lit Zeus' eyes. "Just sayin'."

"Keep out of it, Odysseus. I will show this boy up for the troublemaker he is." Zeus swirled the dark, muddy liquid in his mug thoughtfully. "Jax, you will challenge him to that charity football match. I have arranged it with the Hellenics. Coach Maradona and I go way back to the days of e*piskyros,* a far more superior game than the one they play today. He'll go away and lick his wounds at the loss when he finds a better player than himself. Losers don't like attention."

"And the point of that is?" As much as Arian wanted Craig to slink away into the hole he'd dug for himself, she knew him well enough to know that he'd soon get bored with the subject and drop it anyway. All it would take was distraction in a feminine form. Challenging him to a game he would no doubt win was asking for trouble and not the ideal way to stay out of the media spotlight.

Zeus grinned. "A little fun for the boys here, some muscle-flexing and a good workout will do them good. The thing is McMahon has never been challenged before. He gets his own way with everything because he is spoiled by talent and money. Money cannot buy you everything, especially not a woman. Nor can it buy love and affection. He needs to learn to lose."

Fun for the boys? At her expense? All this talk of challenges, war and battles … on top of everything that had happened since she and Penny had set foot on Paradise Beach … a cauldron of emotions bubbled to the surface and Arian didn't bother pushing them down. Fury boiled within her. She was damned if she would be used like some bloody bartering tool for their pleasure. If they wanted to make a spectacle of themselves and give Craig the satisfaction of winning the attention he so desperately sought, they were on their own.

"I'm not for sale." Arian tipped her chin and straightened her back, shoulders squared. "And I'm not a prize to be dangled between two idiots."

Pain and humiliation rolled through her. Was that all she'd ever be — a pretty accessory on a man's arm, a trophy to be won in a battle between two boofheads? Is that what awaited her as Queen of Paradise too? Was that Zeus' plan?

Gran had asked him to find her so he'd seen his chance and took it. He'd sent his chieftain to guard her, the same man who'd accompany her to war for her queendom … it all made sense now. She'd bet her last dollar they *had* drugged her ambrosia, made her fall in love with Jax. By her side, he'd be king and Zeus would have his slice of Paradise.

The bitterness of betrayal bubbled in her throat as the smell of sulphur reached her nose. *They're playing you for a fool.* The whisper of a voice in her mind had her nerves coiling like an overwound spring. Damned if the voice wasn't right … and that hurt more than the hand squeezing her heart.

Jax's hand tightened around hers and squeezed. "Arian —"

Anger blazed in her belly and lit her eyes with green fire. "You can all go to hell." Her throat closed around the words as she pushed his hand off her shoulder, stood, and shoved her chair back hard so it fell with a clang on the tiled floor. "I'm leaving. Come, Penny, let's go home."

Zeus drained the liquid from his mug, giving it a little

shake so the last drop coated his tongue. "I'm afraid you can't do that, Your Highness."

Her heart pounding so hard it ached, Arian stopped halfway to the kitchen door and turned. "I'll do what I damned well like. I don't know what drugs you lot are on, but I don't need to believe all this bullshit about Faerie Queens and Paradise, no matter what I dreamt and read last night. If you want to have a pissing contest with Craig McMahon, go ahead. Leave me out of it. I was done with that arsehole long before he stirred up this media storm. I have no idea why he's doing it or who's putting him up to it, but I can assure you, I damn well will find out." She marched up to Zeus, so big in his chair she didn't have to lean down to meet him eye to eye. Unperturbed by the twinkle of admiration and humour she saw in the pale grey gaze, she continued. "You don't get to play god in my life."

"Ahh … there's that fighting spirit. Hang on to that fire, Your Highness. You're going to need it soon."

"Screw you. I'm done." She turned and walked away.

Zeus pushed back his chair, the legs scraping the floor under his weight. "Arian ..."

"What?" Her back stiff with fury and her head pounding with tension, she pressed a hand to her heaving stomach. Her heart ached as her illusion of love shattered and emptiness took its place. Men really were egotistical, facetious, testosterone-driven bastards after all.

Zeus stepped towards her, his big, heavy hand gentle on her shoulder. "I know all this is hard to take in. You've had a tumultuous few weeks — months even — but I made a promise to your grandmother and I don't go back on my word." He turned her to face him, gigantic above her petite figure, and raised her chin with his finger. "If you don't go back and save Paradise, Hades will destroy it with crime and pollution. Your people need you. They are without leadership and their land is dying. Do you want to see an entire nation depleted? People without homes, jobs, food? Will your heart allow that, my Faerie Queen?"

No, the picture he painted wasn't a pretty one, but she wasn't a faerie or a queen, she was Arian Kendrick, owner of Kendrick Surveying, the blood in her veins red, not green. *Believe the unbelievable ... always.* Gran's voice in her mind made her waver a moment.

"And if I don't follow your orders?"

"You die."

"How do I look?" Zeus asked as he adjusted the black jacket on his shoulders and fiddled with the knot in his tie. He looked more like Santa than a powerful lawyer, but Arian wasn't game to tell him that.

"Like a man who knows what he's talking about," she said instead.

"I'd be more bloody comfortable in my robes." He peeked out the window at the crowd gathered around the steps of Melbourne's courthouse. "Looks like my tweets worked. We even have a few picketers."

"I thought you hated Earth's technology," grumbled Odys.

"I do, but Twitter is like a carrier pigeon so I understand it. Beats those mouldy old scrolls any day. I might have to introduce it when I get back."

"Let's get out there and do this." Jax pulled at the sleeves of his blue business shirt. "You look beautiful, my darling Arian. I am proud to go out there with you by my side."

Arian did a little twirl, the sweep of her aqua Grecian styled knee length dress full against her bare legs, the pearl and diamante beadwork sparkling under the lights inside the courthouse foyer. An outfit fit for a queen who owned a slice of Paradise. She still struggled with that news, but after everything that had happened since Mykonos she was prepared to view the proof before reaching any conclusions. When the media conference was over, the harpies would be waiting at the house in Oakleigh to sweep them away to the realm within which her future lay.

After she'd lost her temper with them earlier, Helen had come to her and explained it more clearly than Zeus had, and she couldn't argue with the reasoning. When she'd told Helen her theory of why Zeus had sent Jax as her bodyguard, she'd simply smiled, shook her head and said, "Zeus always has a plan but there are some things he lets fate deal with. Love and marriage are two of those things because fate doesn't trust Zeus' judgement."

Scepticism dogged her thoughts. Zeus had painted an ugly picture of the state of Paradise and the horror that awaited them. Fear crept up her spine like a serpent as a whiff of sulphur burned her nostrils.

"Very Audrey Hepburn," offered Penny, distracting her from her thoughts. "Love what Helen's done with your hair, all swept up in that elegant do. Oh my God, are those real diamonds in that clip?"

"From Zeus' own collection." Jax tucked a loose spiral curl behind Arian's ear. "And you wear them beautifully."

She slipped her hand into his and squeezed his fingers as Zeus led the way to where the press waited. Odys,

Penny and Helen brought up the rear. No sooner had they moved through the door than questions were tossed their way, creating a cacophony. Jax squeezed her hand and strength zoomed down Arian's spine, setting it ramrod straight and giving her regal bearing. She stood on the steps of the courthouse, feeling every bit a queen, glad she'd chosen to stand at Jax's side and face down the media accusations in a beautiful dress that made her worthy of her royal title and girlfriend to a god.

A part of her felt sorry for Craig. All this was so far out of his realm of thinking. Hell, a month ago it was out of *her* realm too, but the more she'd questioned Zeus at the breakfast table the clearer it became that Arian Kendrick was more than just a WAG and geographical surveyor. It would take a while to come to grips with the fact that she owned a slice of Paradise, that somewhere in another realm, her queendom waited. With that realisation came a zap of power, a strength she didn't recognise and a gift she had no idea what to do with. Zeus had reassured her Jax would be there to help her hone her skills, and she hoped for her grandmother's sake she could master them before she faced the least star-like demon of all … Hades.

Zeus held up his hand to silence the crowd and no-one questioned his authority. A hush fell below them.

"In response to the allegations made by the Demons' forward, Craig McMahon, I would like it known that Ajax Polemistis and Odysseus Laertiades do indeed exist and neither are the scoundrels they are being made out to be. They are both law abiding citizens of Melbourne with links that go back to the first settlers in this country."

Zeus fielded questions for a while as he laid each doubt to rest with proof. Somehow he'd even managed to produce a few witnesses who could testify that Jax had indeed defended them in court and others who swore they'd partied in Odys' bar. As the crowd began to disperse, Craig McMahon stepped forward.

"You might have fooled the public. You haven't fooled me."

"Give it up, McMahon." Jax turned to follow Zeus inside.

"You have something that belongs to me and I won't leave without it."

The stragglers sensed a fight and stopped to watch as Jax turned, and slowly walked down the steps towards Craig.

Arian followed and laid a hand on his sleeve to stop him. "Ignore him, Jax, please."

Craig snarled at her. "Look at you, all pimped up like a whore. That's all you'll ever be, Arian — a trophy, a bit of bling and bum fluff. You're living in a fantasy world where you'll never belong. You'll always be the one I cast off."

Arian's head spun as the sulphur she'd smelled earlier reached in, making her dizzy and nauseous. "Jax … it's not —"

He squeezed her hand. "Trust me, my love. You go inside with the others and I'll take care of our friend here." She hesitated a moment and he stroked her cheek with a gentle hand. "Go, I'll deal with him."

Panic squeezed her throat. Did Jax know? "Jax, that's not Craig," she whispered.

He frowned but said nothing as he nudged her towards the courthouse. *Trust me.*

Arian nodded and walked to where Zeus had paused to wait for her.

Jax waited until the doors of the courthouse swished closed behind them before he turned back to face Craig. "Arian is not a possession. She is a woman with a mind of her own who deserves more respect than you give."

Craig snorted. "Not much between those ears, my friend. She's not much good in the sack either." The few people around them gasped at the insult.

Jax smiled patiently at him, refusing to bite. McMahon's arrogance would be his downfall as Zeus kept reminding him of his own, he thought, as even the picketers backed away, physically withdrawing their support of the Demons' star player. If he'd learnt anything over the years in Purgatory, it was that arrogance gained you nothing but false security. "What will it take to make you go away?"

Craig narrowed his eyes, his smile smug. "Is that a threat or a bribe? On national television? I can see the Twitter posts now ..."

"Here's an idea," said Jax, ignoring the jab. "If we win the game on Saturday, you walk away. Stop this infernal haranguing by the press and leave Arian in peace."

"What? You're playing the charity match? I didn't see your name on the playlist."

"Ah, it looks like your coaches may have forgotten to mention the game change. You see, the Redbacks had to pull out due to injuries. You're playing against the Hellenics … and me."

"They can't do that." Craig's face flushed, anger radiating in his stance.

"They have."

"Since when do you play football? You don't even exist. This is all some scam, I can prove it."

Jax scowled at him and Craig took a small step back. "You can prove nothing. My lawyer has delivered a sworn statement to the press, and the details of my practice and law degree are listed on the National Register of Legal Practitioners. So, unless you want to find yourself in court on charges of harassment and defamation — back off. Your little attention-seeking game has backfired, McMahon. Arian doesn't want you, and you'll never be the world's next big football star. You couldn't come close to such skilled perfection. Now, do we have a deal?"

Craig hesitated and then smiled broadly. "You're on. Hellenics are at the bottom of the league ladder. It'll be an easy win. Tell Arian to pack her bags, she's coming home with me on Saturday, because when she sees me trample your arse on that field, she won't want to know you. That girl likes the spotlight more than I do. I can make her famous. What can you do for her?"

If only the stupid little prick had a clue … Jax grinned and took his satisfaction from the look of frustration on Craig's face. "I guess I'll see you on the field." He acknowledged Hades with a nod, where he stood behind Craig disguised as a reporter clearly in control of the footballer's mind.

"See you in hell," said Hades.

Jax smiled. If a game of football was Hades' idea of a battle, he was in for a surprise when they arrived in Paradise.

CHAPTER TWELVE

"Why can't Craig leave it be? I've never seen him so nasty — arrogant, self-absorbed and egotistical, definitely, but not mean like he was today." Arian stood with Penny on the patio of the home in Oakleigh and sipped a goblet of Zeus' brew.

"Must have something up his butt because he's like a dog with a bone lately, he just won't let go. He's an attention-seeker, yes. He always has been. You were too blinded by his charm to see it. Maybe he's finally showing his true colours."

Under cover of dark, the harpies had come out to play. Arian wished she could feel the same joy and freedom as they laughed and frolicked about, careful to keep their wings hidden from view. To anyone wanting to spy over the fence or dense hedges, they would look like normal human beings wearing shawls against the night chill.

Unease crawled up her spine, their whole situation totally out of her comfort zone, despite the acceptance in her heart. She scanned the topographical geography of

Earth from the safety of a Cessna 172 Skyhawk, not from the saddle on a harpy. Yet here she was sipping magical potion, watching the mystical creatures play, and holding an audience with the great god himself who was currently in a closed door meeting with Ajax the Great, Odysseus and Helen of Troy, discussing secret squirrels' business. *Helen of Troy*, for God's sake.

"Am I just as blind this time around? Are you seeing what I'm seeing here, Penny?"

Penny shrugged. "I'm the one who should be having doubts. I'm the mortal here. Deep down, you know this is real. You've never felt like you belong here, Arian. Your gran always said you were more fey than she was."

"Gran was old and forgetful near the end. One day she was the Faerie Queen, seeing her minions dancing around her in a ring, calling her home. The next she was simply Rhoda, the aromatherapist from Caer Sidi. What if Zeus is wrong?"

"You don't believe that any more than I do." Penny put down her drink to hug Arian's shoulders. "Remember the tea she used to brew whenever we got a cold or a tummy ache? It worked to make us feel better and take the pain away every time, and now we know why. She was a special lady with special powers."

"Yes, she was. I guess I simply didn't recognise them as magic. I wish she were here now. I could really do with some guidance, some confirmation that this —" Arian waved her hand towards the harpies, "— isn't hereditary madness."

"I'm seeing the same as you are, so either this is one potent brew or we really are hobnobbing with the gods of

Olympus." Penny moved away to pour another drink — water this time.

Arian giggled. "Well, when you say it like that ..." With a sigh, she put down her glass. "I guess I just want confirmation that this is real … that Jax is real."

Strong arms wrapped around her waist from behind and she squealed as Jax drew her tightly against his chest. The brush of his light beard against her neck made her shiver with pleasure even as her heart pounded with love.

"I have no problem proving I am very, very real," he whispered in her ear. "But first, I have Zeus' permission to show you something." Jax stepped away and she missed the solid reality of his warm, hard body against hers. "Come."

Her hand clasped tightly in his, he led her inside, along a corridor and into the garage. Shaking his head, he pushed aside the clutter of the twin harpies' beds. "Typical teenagers, they never make their beds. If only they were as tidy as their mother."

He pulled a device from the belt of his jeans that looked like an ancient key but instead of inserting it in a lock … he drew a square on the floor of the garage. An area the size of a manhole glowed orange in the dull light of the moon that shone through the little window on the wall. It opened to reveal a staircase spiralling downwards into darkness.

"I'll go first. Stay close behind me. The stairs are steep and we have quite a way to go down."

Arian nodded, hitched a finger through a loop on his jeans, ready to stick as close as she could to him. For a moment she questioned her sanity again. What if this was a trap? Perhaps she trusted him too easily?

Sensing her hesitation, he turned around and she let go of him. *Tell the truth and shame the devil.* Gran's words of wisdom echoed in her thoughts. "I'm scared, Jax," she whispered. "This is all too much to take in."

"Ah, my sweet love," Jax murmured, taking her face gently between his hands and placing a soft, butterfly kiss on her lips. "You have nothing to be afraid of. I could never harm you. You are my heart, my soul, the very breath in my lungs. The only way I can prove beyond reasonable doubt that I am who I say I am is to provide you with tangible evidence."

"That's pure lawyer speak."

Jax chuckled, the sound so sexy against her lips, it quivered through her and set her nerve endings on fire. "No, that's Zeus speak." With a teasing kiss below her ear, he whispered, "I'm under orders from the big man himself."

Arian relaxed against his solid chest and allowed her hands to wander from the waistband of his jeans. "I kinda like him a little too."

"More than me?" He nibbled lightly at her earlobe.

She shivered against him, delighted at the hiss of breath in her ear when her hands reached their target. "You have a much nicer arse," she said, giving it a firm squeeze as she pulled him closer.

He reciprocated by mirroring her move, and kissed her breathless as they balanced precariously above the trapdoor in the floor.

"Oh for the love of Aphrodite, would you two please focus on the task I've set?" Zeus' voice boomed around them. "Get on with it."

Jax withdrew his arms from around her with a grin. "Hold on tight."

Together they made their way down the narrow, winding staircase. Each step lit before them and darkened again as they passed. Arian drove down the need to peer up into the darkness behind her to see if the way out still glowed above. This was a test of trust as much as it was about what lay concealed below, so she tightened her hold on Jax's waist and plucked up courage, the solid feel of his body beneath her hands a comfort.

Finally they reached the bottom. A little light-headed from the descent, Arian swayed against Jax, seeking the stability he provided. Drawing her close, he snapped his fingers and lights flickered to life. Suspended on air and encased in a protective force field, the exquisite workmanship of the armour before her stole the remaining breath from Arian's lungs.

"The Shield of Achilles," she whispered.

The air around them pulsed with a power the force field could not contain. Jax edged her closer and the pulsing grew stronger, as if the shield was alive and its heartbeat reached for them.

It shimmered with vibrant and unexpected colour under the light as the force field around it dropped away. Gold, silver and the cyan Arian recognised as coming from the paste created with low-fired glass, the shield was alive with etchings, each with a story to tell.

The centre of the orb drew her attention as she stepped out of Jax's hold. The Mask of Fear stared back at her with empty eyes, gorgon-like teeth bared in a snarl — a warning of danger to come. She shivered and let her gaze wander to the circle of constellations surrounding it instead, and the happier scenes of weddings and dancing.

"My God, Jax, this is awesome. The workmanship in this shield is … incredible. How?" Arian reached out, wanting to run her fingers over the crazy mix of smoothly crafted sheep and bulls, the sweep of the dancers' skirts and the warriors wielding their swords in battle. She held back, knowing the damage body oils could do to ancient artefacts.

"Pure magic, my love." Jax drew her against him and held her tightly. "One day I will tell you each of those stories represented on the shield. It represents everything we have fought to protect — our women, our children, our land and our honour."

His voice vibrated with pride and Arian closed her eyes to listen, absorbing the timbre and depth of it, the warmth of his arms as they banded her waist and the strength in the lines of his body. No-one could possibly fake such pride in telling Achilles' story, his gruesome death, unless they had truly been there to witness it. The pain in Jax's voice told of the loss of more than a friend and fellow god — he'd lost a brother.

Arian turned in his arms, her hands splayed on his chest as she listened. His eyes were on the shield as he spoke, seeing something she couldn't. She reached up to stroke his jaw, his beard soft and comforting against her palm, the movement of his lips mesmerising. In that moment she knew for certain … this man was her soul mate, the one Gran had promised would come for her.

She stilled his lips with her fingers, drawing in a breath when he pressed a kiss against the tips. "I believe."

One hand in the small of her back, the other pressing

her hand to his heart, he kissed her, sweetly, tenderly, with the smallest hint of the passion they would share later alone in their room.

"Save me, Arian. Save me from the purgatory I have endured these thousands of years, from the clutches of Hades who snaps at my heels," he said, lifting his head, his green gaze pleading with hers.

"How do I do that?"

"By loving me and making me whole."

"I can do that." Arian kissed the pulse that beat at the base of his neck, revealed in the vee of his shirt. Her hands slipped up under the material to touch the warm skin of his body. Her fingers traced the scar on his chest. She knew the cause of it now.

"Enough." Zeus appeared from nowhere, snapped his fingers and the force field drew up around the shield once more. "It is not as simple as only loving each other. There is work to do yet. Paradise awaits its queen. We need to prepare for battle."

Arian bit her lip. Her biggest battle yet had been for shoes in her size at the Boxing Day sales. What did she know about battle strategies and swordfights?

"You really need to trust your own strength and abilities, Arian. Paradise can't have a queen with trust issues. I have your grandmother's weapons in the safe upstairs. I'll need to show you how to use them." Zeus eyed the circular staircase with disdain. "No bloody way I'm going up that thing. You two are on your own. Meet me upstairs." Then he was gone.

Below them, the Earth was dark. From the sky above, the twinkle of streetlights formed dotted patterns on the landscape. Sitting behind Jax on Electra's back, she touched the Celtic war sword — with its black wooden grip and silver half-moon guard and pommel — in the sheath at her side. It hummed with power at her touch.

The moment Zeus had placed it in her hands, it had glowed with a white-blue light and the hilt had moulded into her hand for a perfect fit.

"If you doubted before, Your Highness, there lies the proof. The sword only moulds to the grip of the true Faerie Queen."

She would have liked to deny it, but even as the thought formed, a warm strength had flowed through her, bringing with it a sense of belonging she hadn't felt since Gran died.

As they'd planned their arrival and attack in Paradise, her confidence had grown as she recognised landmarks Gran had mentioned in her book, and the fantasy had turned to reality. A far better, more comfortable reality than she'd ever known.

Jax reached back and squeezed her thigh. "You okay?"

"Yes, just processing."

"You think too much."

Beneath them, Electra dipped to the right and curved towards an island cloaked in semi-darkness below. "Welcome to Leuke. Once it was Paradise." She cruised in to land on a bank of dark red soil where it bled into an empty creek bed. "The dirt is soaked with the blood of those who defended Paradise against Hades."

She crouched so Jax and Arian could climb off. As Arian's

feet touched the soil, green grass began to sprout under them. Fascinated, she took a few steps forward. Beside her a bed of brown, bedraggled plants lifted their heads and bloomed.

"Jax, what's happening?"

He smiled. "It's true. You really are Arianrhod, Restorer of Life and Souls." A roar in the distance followed by a ball of flames shooting skyward caught their attention. "Come, we must hurry to the palace. The water faeries are doing their best to stop Hades from burning the castle. They can't hold off much longer."

They ran through the bush that sprung up around them, swords ready. Ahead, the land was strewn with the whitened bones of those who'd battled with the devil and lost. With a sweep of her sword, Arian raised their souls from the dirt as she went. A war cry lifted behind her as they followed, gathering life as they went.

Arian felt her power grow along with her confidence as they reached the village outside the castle wall. With only a few thatched cottages left standing on the blackened earth, the destruction tore at her heart. These were *her* people who'd suffered and she would have no more of it. She shook off the pain of devastation as pride and determination seeped into her soul, stiffening her spine and squaring her shoulders to give her the regal bearing and strength she needed. Her sword sang as she raised it to the sky.

"Hades, you miserable son of a bitch, get your lousy arse out here now and face me like the devil you are," she roared.

"Arian, we must follow the plan —"

"Screw the plan, Ajax. He's already breeched the outer

wall. If any of my people are still alive, they won't be for much longer."

Hades appeared at the battered gates dangling from the hinges, his black cloak billowing around him against a wall of fire. "Oh, God damn it," he yelled. "If it isn't the bloody Welsh witch's offspring. You're too late, Arianrhod. You can't save them now. All I need to do is breathe on them and they'll drop like tenpins." His laughter shook the walls. "You plan to fight me with a bunch of useless ghosts and a coward, Your Highness?"

Rage filled her. She didn't even try to stem it, instead she let it drive her forward. "The only coward here is you, Hades. You trick people, play with their minds, drug them with ouzo — that's not the work of a hero or leader. Fight like a man if you want to own Paradise."

"Oh, you stupid, stupid girl. You are no match for me. I won't waste my strength on anyone except Ajax the Great. Today his soul will be mine and he will become my slave in hell, doing my bidding day and night." He stepped towards them. "Even now, you hide behind the skirts of a woman, you yellow-bellied weakling. Perhaps I should leave you to Athena to finish off? She'd love that, I'm sure."

Jax stepped in front of Arian and pulled her in behind him. "I'll never be your slave." He raised his sword and shield. "But may Zeus be my witness, I will kill you today."

Hades threw back his head and roared. The ground shook and shivered beneath their feet. "Bring it on." He raced forward.

Jax pushed Arian back into the crowd of souls behind them and surged towards Hades, meeting him halfway.

Steel clashed against steel and fire raged around them, building into an impenetrable wall. As they fought, Arian turned to the souls she had raised. They had begun to regrow their bodies.

"Quickly," she called to the ones who'd wholly regenerated, "help the water faeries secure the castle."

"Yes, my queen," they chorused and set off for the drawbridge.

With a growl of pain, Jax flew out of the wall of flames and landed at her feet, battered and lifeless, blood leaking from his side.

"No," shouted Arian, pain tearing through her. She dropped down at Jax's side. Fear and emptiness gripped her, ripping at her heart and eating into her stomach. Jax could not be dead. She loved him, loved him more than anything else in the world.

Hot hands fisted in her hair and dragged her to her feet. Foul sulphur breath grazed her cheek. She retched. The hand tightened, stretched her scalp until she thought he'd rip off her hair along with the top of her head. She eased her sword to her side as he laughed in her ear.

"It's the end of the road, Queenie. Today you die and Paradise is mine to rule. I need somewhere quiet to escape to since hell is so full these days. Your little world is perfect. How about we do a deal, huh?"

"Fuck you," she spat.

His blade touched her throat, nicking it deep enough to bleed. Her blood fell green on the red dirt. "Such spirit. Your grandmother had the same. I had to beat it out of her. Quite a pleasure, really. I'm going to enjoy sending you to the same fate … after I've had a little fun with that delectable little body of yours." He ran a gnarled hand down her side and cupped her bottom, pressing a wet kiss into her exposed neck.

"Never. You killed the man I love. Now I'm going to kill you."

Hades chuckled, an annoying soulless laugh. "Jax never loved you. You Earth people are so gullible with this whole love thing. He used you, sweetheart. That whole Mykonos thing? It was all a lie. Zeus sent him to guard you. The horny bastard couldn't keep it in his pants so he pretended to have the hots for you. There, he could do his job and screw you to the wall while he was at it. Such bad behaviour for a royal — no-one will respect you now. It could have worked out well really. Being married to the Queen of Paradise would entitle you to certain privileges … like how, if something had to happen to you, he'd inherit your queendom. Quite convenient, isn't it? How does that make you feel, My Lady Arian?"

Her eyes watered and her lips trembled as the pain of Hades' grip tore into her skull and his words pierced her soul like shards of broken glass. She fought against the thoughts Hades sought to imbed in her mind. No, Jax loved her. She knew it. She'd seen it in his kiss, when they made love … and even if he didn't — God help her — she loved him more than life.

"He's a god, Arian. His magic knows no bounds. Rumour has it he's had more women than Zeus himself … and that's a lot. He's dead now, and this time he won't rise."

His taunts buzzed in her ears, fed her rage and pain. Bile crept up her throat as she chanted St Patrick's Prayer, her only defence against him.

I bind unto myself today

The virtues of the starlit heavens,
The glorious sun's life-giving ray,
The whiteness of the moon at even,
The flashing of the lightning free,
The whirling wind's tempestuous shocks,
The stable earth, the deep salt sea,
Around the old eternal rocks,
So may it be.

Hades howled in agony as white light engulfed him. He spun away from her, stumbling into a pit dug by her people as their souls regenerated, setting the perfect trap. As he fell, Arian wiped the blood from her neck. She looked down into the tight round hole and found him wedged securely, head down, bum up.

Victory warred with loss. She looked across at Ajax's body, a bloody warrior in death. It no longer mattered if Hades was right or wrong about him loving her. Jax had died a hero, not a coward. As her heart shattered, she gripped the hilt of her sword and raised it high. With a roar of victory, she drove the blade into the devil's arse. Then she wept.

CHAPTER THIRTEEN

"He's awake, Your Highness."

"Thank you, Rhoswen. I'll see him for a moment and then bring him to the balcony, please."

"Of course, Your Highness."

As Hades lay trapped in the pit, Arian had tended Jax's body, dressed his wounds and cleaned him up. The sight of him lifeless was more than she could bear, his skin cold and clammy to touch.

Even Hades' hint at betrayal couldn't kill what she felt for him. If the devil was right, she'd let him go but she couldn't leave him dead. So she'd closed her eyes, laid her hands on his heart and her mouth on his lips then breathed into him all the love she felt.

In battle you bravely fought,
Honour to yourself you brought,
The war is won,
Your time has come,
Step into the unknown,
For you have grown,

In honour, trust and love,
Now I release you from your past,
To begin a new life at last,
So may it be.

Now, a week later, with Hades in the cells waiting for collection by Zeus, Jax was alive. He'd share the moment of victory with her as was his due when she made her first address as queen, then he too would leave with Zeus. She would nurse her broken heart while she rebuilt Paradise and Jax would return to Earth having being cleansed of the guilt and failure he carried on his shoulders.

Gran had always said that if you truly loved someone, you set them free. If they returned to you, it was meant to be. Deep in her heart, she hoped Gran was right because without him she would never be whole.

She pushed open the door to his suite. He lay battered and bruised on the bed. Dark purple marks bloomed around his ribs and kidneys, and the gash in his side was red and raw where Hades' sword had torn into it. Gone was the bronzed hue his naked skin had held so well, and in its place was a canvas of abrasions in varying shades of blue.

"Arian ..." he breathed, his eyes filled with sadness. "I failed you."

His words echoed around the empty chambers of her heart. "You didn't fail me, Jax, you saved Paradise."

He shook his head and groaned, his eyes closing against the pain. "No, I let Hades get to you."

In tune with his mind and body, she felt the extent of his agony and torment with every breath he drew and every word he groaned. True Chieftains never failed — something Jax believed in more than love. Would his infernal pride always control his heart? "And I set you free when I gave you back your life. Zeus will arrive later to take you back to Oakleigh."

"What about you?"

Arian lifted her chin against the sadness threatening to overwhelm her. She too had her pride. "This is my home now. These people need me. You won, Jax. Freedom is yours."

"What do you mean?" He pushed himself up on his elbow, wincing as he did. "I love you, Arian. My life is where you are."

If only that were true her soul would be complete. Whatever sparked between them could not carry the label of love, because lovers didn't lie to each other. She fought through the tightness in her throat.

"You can stop pretending. I know the truth. I know that Zeus employed you to be my bodyguard and that you pretended to be interested in me to serve the purpose. Go home, Ajax the Great. Go and celebrate your victory, your freedom. You are a brave warrior and you have earned your soul to keep. The Shield of Achilles is yours."

She turned away as tears stung her eyes, shoulders stiff, spine straight, hoping she looked like the regal queen she'd accepted she was.

The moment she'd stepped on Paradise soil, she knew she'd truly come home and although she'd commit to her reign, her heart would always be in another time, another place with the same name. The weight of disappointment and heartbreak dragged at her feet as she left the room and the only man she'd ever truly loved.

Closing the door behind her, Arian made her way down the corridor to the balcony. She adjusted the crown of wildflowers on her head and smoothed the layers of her aqua silk dress, then stepped through the great oak doors and into a riot of applause and chants. As she waited, she waved at the crowd. She caught a movement behind her and she knew Jax was there. She closed her eyes against the pain that tore at her, knowing they would soon be separated.

In silence, he stood beside her in his *chitoniskos,* his breast plate cleaned and polished, the Shield of Achilles on his arm. God help her, he was damn sexy in uniform. A surge of love and pride swept through her. The heat from his body warmed her chilled one and she wanted to turn into his side and bury herself there. She couldn't. He'd earned his freedom and she no longer needed protection, so instead she addressed the crowd.

"Good people of Paradise, your life, your land and your hopes are renewed once more. Praise be to Zeus that Ajax the Great could fight by our side and send Hades back to hell." She spread her arms wide. "Many of you sacrificed your own lives in battle and it is my pleasure to have restored you to the living once more. May we go forth in peace."

As the crowd applauded, the sky darkened with a storm and, on the heels of a lightning bolt, Zeus' chariot descended. Arian shook her head. If it wasn't for the skill of the harpies, the chariot would topple at the speed he landed.

He climbed out of the chariot and was led up to join them on the balcony.

"Arian, dear child, you did it. The place looks beautiful. The sun is shining, the grass is greener than it's ever been and the flowers are blooming again." Zeus kissed her cheeks. "And Ajax … I thought you were dead?"

The muscles in Jax's cheeks flinched as he tightened his jaw. Arian could no longer feel what he was feeling. He'd closed his heart and mind to her.

Zeus' eyes narrowed as he studied first Jax then Arian. He shook his head but said nothing.

"Hades is waiting in the cells below, Zeus. When you are ready to leave, I will have him delivered to the chariot. He's having a little trouble walking."

Zeus chuckled. "I always said he was a pain in the arse."

Arian's lips twitched. "You are so bad. Come, let's have a drink to celebrate our victory then you can be on your way."

"Are you not accompanying us back to Earth? Paradise can surely spare you for a day or two now they're no longer under threat? I thought you'd like to see the Hellenics kick some Demon Dodgers arse."

"Call off the match. It's no longer necessary and I have no need to see it either. Hades had control of his mind, not that it excuses his behaviour prior to these events. Humility was never his strong point. Craig McMahon no longer means anything to me because I will not return to Earth. My people need me. They have been without leadership for far too long."

"Your Highness, if I may say so, your people will be happily feasting and drinking to your success for days to come. They won't even know if you pop out for a few days to celebrate with Penny and the rest of us. Besides, the match is for a good cause. I have no reason to call it off. If I do, the charity won't receive the funds it so desperately needs for research. Could you, as queen, deny a child the right to a cure?"

No, what remained of her heart wouldn't allow it. In her selfishness, she'd forgotten the true reason behind the match. She did miss Penny, and perhaps if she did go back for the football match she could bring Penny back to Paradise for a while. But spending all that time in Jax's company, knowing she loved him with all her heart and he didn't love her in the same way, would be more than she could bear.

"Why don't you leave Electra here for me and I'll get there in time for the match? I would like to get to know my people a little better before I leave again, if only for a short while."

Zeus looked between Ajax and Arian. "You two have to be the most stubborn beings I've met, not to mention blind, but we'll do it your way. I will take Ajax and Hades with me now. Jax, you have a game to play. We need to make sure you're well-rested." He looked squarely at the two of them standing so close together yet so far apart and shook his head. "Blind, I tell you, blind."

Strapped to the front of the chariot, Hades swore revenge with each jerk and twist of the journey to Earth. Jax ignored his taunts, his mind with Arian in Paradise. Zeus was right, he was blind. Victory was bittersweet without her. Yes, he'd lied, pretended his interest at first, but somewhere between Paradise Beach and Oakleigh he'd lost his heart. His mistrust of women had diminished as he'd grown to know Arian for the tender-hearted creature she was. Not once had she tried to deceive him or betray him. Even though he'd failed to save her from Hades and she had proven herself a warrior in conquering the evil that had taken hold on Paradise, she'd shared the triumph with him, held him up a hero. He didn't deserve an iota of that pride.

Waking up with her in his bed had made his soul more resilient, his heart softer. With each touch, each kiss, he'd grown stronger, his heart beat more regularly. Coming back to life felt damn good but owning a soul without a heart was useless. She'd completed the restoration of his body and mind, making him whole once more. He should be happy he'd achieved his pardon, his goal to live again, yet all he felt was emptiness without her by his side. Without her, he may as well be dead because this sure as hell wasn't living.

All he needed to do was win the football game, a battle with no purpose except for one-upmanship against a vain and weak enemy, but a battle nonetheless, if only to quiet the press and teach a man a lesson in humility. One he'd learned himself only hours before.

Ownership of the Shield of Achilles no longer mattered. He'd found a treasure far more valuable, and had lost it through his own ignorance. He'd fought and lost battles over women before on Olympus. None had left him feeling as bereft as he was without Arian. The stakes were higher this time. Suffering the humiliation of another failure would be minimal when measured against thousands more years without her.

McMahon would fight dirty and he was prepared for that. The battle was no longer over Arian, it was a matter of pride and teaching the snivelling twit a lesson.

"It's for a good cause. Not even on Olympus is there a cure for cancer, so the event is an important fundraiser." Zeus interrupted his musings. "You need to mentally prepare for the battle ahead. The game of football is as strategic as any battle you've fought before — attack and defence — except the weapon was a ball not a sword and shield. A single point has to be fought hard for, the moves planned carefully around the opposition's game play. Odys will have your back at all times, just as he had at the Battle of Troy."

Yes, he could always count on Odysseus, something he'd lost sight of at the Battle of Troy and hadn't needed in the fight for Paradise. There Arian had his back. Greed was an unforgiving taskmaster and he'd let it rule his head. In one last selfless deed, he would give this match his all for charity and for Arian, who deserved so much better than an egotistical footballer or an arrogant god in her life. Then he'd walk away to wander the land as he had for the last two thousand years, his soul empty and his heart lost, until he died a mortal.

Zeus sat in the first row behind midfield, Helen to the left with Ermioni between her, Arian and Penny. He settled in with his smartphone ready to tweet the game — #thechallenge. Wearing the Hellenics supporters' guernsey, he knew he fitted in perfectly with the crowd. He shivered a little as someone large settled into the seat on the other side of him and heard Helen's sharp intake of breath. *Not good.*

"Hades, how's your arse healing?" he said, sarcasm

weighing heavily in his tone. "To what do we owe this displeasure? Didn't I warn you to stay away?"

He looked at the being on his right. Hades was suited up for business rather than leisure. The expensive suit and jet-black hair, sleeked back, did little to soften his harsh, angular features. He smoothed the carefully manicured goatee on his chin with long graceful fingers ringed with gold. Zeus understood how women fell for his dark handsomeness, not knowing the evil that lurked beneath until too late.

"Nothing sulphur paste won't fix. It's great for sealing open wounds. Burns like shit but it gets the job done." Flicking a speck of stray ash from the lapel of his jacket, he grinned. "I'm here to claim the soul you've kept from hell. I have waited long enough, caused enough of a kafuffle."

"I should have known you were behind the media crap. How did you coerce Craig McMahon into going along with your little farce — staging the proposal, picketing outside the courthouse, the WAGs' Twitterfit?"

"Mortals are so vain," said Hades, smoothing a hand over his gelled hair. "McMahon's ego made him an easy target. He'd do anything for a spot in the proverbial limelight — so bloody boringly predictable and so damn easy to take control of." He studied his neatly clipped nails, blew on the tips, and polished them against the lapel of his jacket. "So … when can I take my boy home?"

"You're too late. The healing has begun." Zeus brushed him off with more confidence than he felt.

"I am never too late. He's given in to the darkness already. It won't be long before he takes his own life again. I can wait."

"Stay away from him."

"Come now, don't be like that, old man." Hades chuckled, the sound holding no warmth or humour. "The Faerie Queen is very pretty. A lot like her grandmother."

"Leave Arianrhod out of this. You had no right to steal her fey and you won't take Arian's either."

"What woman can resist my charms? I keep myself well, unlike some who have grown … podgy and comfortable." Hades cast a pointed look at Zeus' belly.

"Screw you. If I have to endure your company, please be quiet. The game is about to begin. This is one soul you won't be taking away today."

"We'll see about that."

The Demons won the toss and chose their goal. Odys and Jax lined up in centre field ten metres from the ball and waited for the whistle to blow. Odys kicked off and Jax drove the ball forward, only to be met by resistance from Craig. The arrogant tosser was in his face, taunting, testing his patience, and playing a dirty game. Jax wanted to plant him squarely on his arse but this was a battle that deserved skill and sportsmanship, so he performed Maradona's *tiki-taka* move, and between him and Odys they performed a series of short passes that had McMahon crying foul.

The crowd booed and the referee called, "No foul, play on."

McMahon amped up his attack. He shifted into open spaces left by the Hellenics, approaching the goal using his wingers, and attempting to feed the ball to strikers. Jax shadowed him, waiting for an opportunity to seize the ball. In the moment it took McMahon to look for an open pass, Jax stole the ball and drove it to midfield and beyond.

Anger flared as McMahon gave chase, fisted his hand on Jax's shirt and yanked. Jax stumbled while McMahon fell. The referee blew the whistle to stop play, and held up a yellow card for McMahon. The crowd cheered, McMahon swore and Jax shrugged it off.

For the next forty minutes there might as well only have been three players on the field, when the ball never made it past midfield. McMahon took every opportunity to abuse Jax who ignored the taunts completely.

The half-time whistle blew and Jax jogged over towards the sidelines, hesitating only slightly when he spotted the figure sitting next to Zeus. His glance slid to Zeus and Jax raised an eyebrow. Hades. Jax wondered how much money he'd bet at office to see him lose and what the odds were.

Curious, Arian followed Jax's gaze and studied the dark man in the suit. Cold, empty eyes met hers and she sensed a deep-seated evil in his being. Shivering, she tore her gaze away. Hatred for Hades boiled in her blood. Zeus had promised to keep him away — another broken promise. What was Zeus playing at? As determined as Hades was to take Jax's soul, he shouldn't be allowed anywhere near them.

Arian … Catching her gaze, Jax's voice reached for her mind. *Please, be careful.*

She tucked her hands under her bottom to stop herself

standing up and reaching for him, knowing she'd lose more of her heart if she touched him.

Promise me you'll stay away from him. After his humiliation in Paradise, he'll be looking for revenge.

She frowned. *It's no business of yours, Ajax the Great. I have my own powers to fall back on.* Rejecting him splintered her soul and made her eyes sting with tears. Weakness was the devil's playground, and she was damned if she'd let him take advantage of her sorrow in losing her soul mate.

Hurt and shame flickered in Jax's eyes as he held her gaze. *Even so, stick close to Helen and Zeus. Don't leave them at any cost. They will protect you from his powers. Stay safe.*

For a moment Arian closed her eyes and imagined his hand cupping her cheek, pretending he really cared, because she would never feel his touch on her skin again. *I will. Now go kick some Demons arse.*

He ran off to join the team, leaving Arian even more curious about Hades' presence at the game. Cold fear gripped her spine and panic flooded her mind. He'd come for Jax. She'd saved his life for nothing, cleansed his soul and set him free, only to die again by Hades' hands.

The second half began with less monopolisation of the ball by the three men, and Arian suspected the referees had had a word with the coaches.

"Does our lovely queen know what is truly at stake here?" The dark man's voice lifted above the calls of the crowd to reach Arian's ears.

"Shut up, you fool," growled Zeus.

"She doesn't? Oh my, what a dangerous game you play, old man."

Arian frowned. Jax's warning not to engage him echoed in her head and she forced her attention back to where Odys had driven the ball close enough to the goal to aim a kick, only to be blocked by the Demons. The crowd groaned in frustration and Zeus' response was drowned out.

"Excuse me, my dear."

The voice, dark and thick and sinful as chocolate, reached for Arian as the crowd quieted. She felt the pull of it reaching into her mind, drawing her attention until Helen broke the spell by leaning across and touching her hand.

"Ignore him. Focus on the game," she said aloud and the man chuckled.

"That's not going to help, my lovely Helen."

"I'm not your lovely anything, you slime."

He clicked his tongue. "Careful, my dear. Tis not so long ago you committed your crimes and I might take home your soul instead."

Arian shivered at the threat. Terror, sharp as the blade of Jax's sword, pierced her stomach. There were so many ways he could carry out his evil promise, so many people who could be hurt or killed in the process.

"That's enough," roared Zeus. "Hades, if you can't behave and have the decency to wait for an outcome without throwing the match, please bugger off."

Arian looked at Penny, who was too busy watching Odys to notice the man who'd joined them. Perhaps she couldn't see him. Black thoughts edged into her mind, wisps of evil and doubt.

The feeling of unease that had dogged her since meeting the gods crept back into the pit of Arian's stomach. *You are my heart, my soul, the very breath in my lungs*. Jax's words echoed in her head. She looked out onto the field and found him in the scuffle of bodies as they fought over the ball in the Demons' half. *I'm a descendant of the Welsh goddess Arianrhod, the Queen of Reincarnation.*

Unease grew to full blown nausea as pieces of the last few weeks began to fall together like pieces of a badly cut jigsaw puzzle. *Arianrhod, Faerie Queen and Restorer of Souls. I'm glad I saved yours tonight.*

Jax broke away from the pack, drove the ball down the field and with a hefty kick, sent it flying past the defence and through the middle post. The crowd roared and leapt to their feet, cheering. Arian saw nothing as the sense of betrayal pushed aside the fear and crept into her heart. *Save me, Arian. Save me from the purgatory I have endured these thousands of years, from the clutches of Hades who snaps at my heels.*

She looked across at the dark man who'd also remained seated as the crowd had risen to its collective feet. He looked back at her with a sly smile.

"He used you, my dear." His lips moved but she heard the smooth voice in her head. "He pretended to love you to save his soul, not to protect you as he was elected to. A soul a coward does not deserve to keep."

Pain, sharp as a hot knife, stabbed at her heart. "No."

The crowd stamped on the concrete steps in the upper stadium and cheered as the action on the field heated up.

"It's true, and deep down … you know it." Hades' smile was smug now, the seeds of doubt sewn and beginning to bloom.

"He showed me the Shield of Achilles."

Hades shrugged. "His reward for saving Paradise,

keeping you alive for long enough to claim the throne. A payment that has nothing to do with love and everything to do with avarice."

"You're lying. It doesn't matter anyway. When the game is over, I return to my throne a queen and Jax will live forever in peace on Earth."

"On the contrary, my dear, today is his last day here because I will take control of Earth. Keep your little parcel of Paradise. Humans are far more gullible than faerie folk. Eventually I will rule the universe." The crowd screamed, and chanted the Hellenics team song as Jax took the match to a three goal win over the Demons. "You, my dear, are simply another trophy, a means to an end, the giver of immortality, a tool I will save until the last good spirit falls."

Craig McMahon sank to his knees on the field, head in his hands, playing to his fans as the cameras panned in on him while the Hellenics danced around the field and high-fived the spectators leaning over the fence. The cheers rose to a roar as a tinny voice announced the final score over the loudspeaker. "The Hellenics take the game in a record win ..."

"That's my cue. This will be the last victory your god sees. Don't waste any more effort on him. Say goodbye, my dear. He doesn't have much time left."

Excitement raised the roof of the stadium, fans cried and screamed around her, but for Arian time stood still and none of those sounds made the journey from her ear to her senses. Everything Hades said made sense. She'd been so blinded by the intensity of her feelings for Jax, so swept up in the magic of his loving, that she'd failed to see it. He needed her for nothing more than to live again. Confusion, anger, hurt swirled through her, a tsunami of emotions that confused the truth with the lies.

Her throat closed around the anger and bitterness that rose. In her mind, Hades' voice chanted, "Fool."

Once again, Arian Kendrick had been manipulated, she thought. Just like Craig had used her then cast her aside, Jax would do the same. Zeus' words rang in her ears.

This is my chance to pay your grandmother back, Arian. To make things right, to give you the piece of Paradise that should have been hers, and to present you with the gift of immortality so you may share it with the man who deserves a soul.

What angered her more than the thought of Jax's betrayal was that Hades had stolen Gran's life, her happiness. She was damned if she'd let him do the same to her or Jax, no matter what his crime, not when she'd fought so hard to save him.

Zeus sat down, exhausted and hoarse at the victory. He looked around for Hades and found the seat next to him empty. *Headcount.* Helen, Ermioni, Penny … "Oh, shit."

CHAPTER FOURTEEN

Arian ran hard to catch up with the devil. Ahead she saw Hades strolling along, taunting her with looks cast over his shoulder, laughing insanely.

"Truth or lies, my dear ..." he taunted.

"I won't let you steal his soul, you rotten coward, nor will I let you take control of Earth."

"Who's going to stop me? You?"

"I did once and I will again."

"Ah, but my earthly powers are far stronger. I made it easy for you up there. Down here, I'm the king. Look around you, girl. Everywhere in this world there is evil. Murderers, rapists, thieves and terrorists … your sickly goodness is outweighed here. Go back to Paradise and enjoy it while you can."

Arian reached inside her cape for her sword, the hilt moulding into her hand, the blade ringing with power. She muttered her chant but Hades kept moving, the only sign he'd heard it a roll of his shoulders as he shook off the magic.

He waved at her as he boarded the bus that waited to transport supporters away after the game. She followed, knowing that whatever he planned, she couldn't let innocent people suffer in the wake of his destruction. Disgruntled Demons fans had already almost filled it, muttering their disappointment at the loss.

"Get off the bus," she yelled, raising her sword. Power flashed from the blade, taking out the overhead lights.

"Oh, don't make me kill you, Your Highness." Hades sighed. "I'm not in the mood for messy business."

The crowd fought to get off the bus, pushing Hades aside. In the crush Arian lost sight of him. As soon as the aisles were cleared, the bus jerked and pulled away. The passengers at least were safe. She and Hades were alone, and she would put all her powers into stopping his plans even if it killed her.

The bus swayed around the corner onto La Trobe Street. Arian braced herself against the seat in front. She looked across at the familiar figure in the driver's seat. Hades looked back and smiled, sharp yellow teeth bared, his eyes cold and empty, the neatly combed, jet-black hair replaced with a flaming halo.

"Why?" She braced her legs against the sway of the bus and faced him, her sword clenched at her side.

"Why what?"

"Why did you steal Gran's fey, her immortality?"

"She betrayed me, just like your chieftain betrayed you. She told me she loved me, and then she married your grandfather, the brave soldier, the war-time hero. We could have been good together. Her white magic and my black."

"How could Gran love a man like you? Her heart was pure and yours is as black as coal."

Hades accelerated through an intersection at the same time as a tram whistle screamed a warning, continued through two red lights leaving screeching tyres, crunching metal and smashing glass in his wake.

"My heart wasn't always black, my dear. Love destroyed me and your grandmother was the cause. Now you will suffer the same fate, sacrifice peace and happiness to pay for her mistake."

"I already have. I have nothing more to lose. Leave Ajax to live out his life in peace and take me instead."

Arian raised her sword and called upon its power. The blade glowed blue-white against the darkness inside the bus, a cool contrast to the red flames surrounding Hades.

"I have no use for your soul, Arianrhod. Its purity is a hazard to my plans, a flaw, if you will. But Ajax the Great … his soul is tortured thanks to dear Athena, his mind already twisted. It wouldn't take much to turn him to the dark side. Not this time ..."

The intersection at Harbour Esplanade loomed fast. Clutching the back of the seat, Arian said, "You'll kill me anyway."

"Oh yes, my dear, and you will not rise again. You'll drown just like your brother did when you couldn't find the courage to save him. I tried so hard to get rid of the both of you even then. Eliminating the Faerie Queen's offspring should have been simple. You father was so easy to manipulate. Just like Ajax, he was weak with greed, wanted everything your grandmother owned, so he stood by and let your brother drown. The idiot couldn't find it in himself to murder you too, so I killed him."

Memories flashed through Arian's mind like a

soundless black and white movie. Her father frozen at the water, her standing on the banks wondering why he watched instead of diving in to save his son … just like Jax had the day Ermioni nearly drowned.

"Yes, my dear. I nearly had you that day but you muttered that stupid curse your grandmother taught you. You have no idea what pain that causes me. Luckily Athena gave me a potion to counteract it this time. She too will have her revenge today."

All their lives they'd been manipulated by the devil. Her whole family was lost to her because of greed for riches and possessions. As greedy as Jax was for the Shield of Achilles … enough that he'd sell his body to keep it.

"Ajax will be devastated, his soul will sink into the dark depths of despair and he'll be mine for the taking. Bait, my dear, that's all you are and all you'll ever be." Hades laughed, loud and harsh.

Arian leapt at him, over the rail between the driver's seat and console. With a roar, she raised her sword ready to strike just as Hades put his foot flat on the accelerator pedal, rattled across the tram tracks, over the cycle path, through the garden and off the edge of Central Pier.

Fear echoed through her as she fell back, hitting her head on the windscreen. Her sword clattered down the aisle as the nose rose and the bus became airborne, seconds before plunging into the freezing water of Victoria Harbour.

Jax jerked back as an invisible cord ripped up his spine and pain spread through his body. His head pounded and fear gripped his throat. The roar of the stadium and celebratory cheers of his teammates faded rapidly as darkness enveloped him. He struggled to keep on his feet but a black force drew him down … down … until the air was almost severed from his lungs.

"Jax?" He felt the grip of Odys' hands under his arms, dragging him back out of the crowd. "What's up, buddy?"

"Arian … dying ..." he choked out.

Then Zeus was beside him and he felt the touch of a bottle to his lips. Liquid dribbled into his mouth and down his throat, clearing the constriction. "That's it, swallow."

"What the hell is going on?" Odys demanded.

"Hades … I think he's taken Arian."

"What? Zeus, you were meant to be keeping an eye on her." Odys yelled angrily above the roar of the chanting crowd.

Zeus shook his head. "Got caught up in the game. Took my eyes off the bastard for two seconds."

Jax coughed and raised his head as sirens screamed outside the stadium. He took the bottle out of Zeus' hands and swallowed the contents in one gulp. Energy and magic poured through him, chasing away the darkness. "We have to find her quickly."

"This is Hades we're talking about. She could be anywhere. Besides, you'll need the Shield of Achilles for protection. Without it, he will kill you."

"There's no time." Blackness hovered at the edge of his vision, and the ripe smell of rotting garbage and sulphur seared his nostrils. With his mind, he searched for

Arian's thoughts. All he heard was the deathly silence interrupted occasionally by the sound of something heavy sinking through water.

"I can't help you then, Jax." The stricken look on Zeus' face gave him no comfort. "I cannot summon the shield here with magic. It's too risky."

"Attention. Your attention please." The loudspeaker rattled at full volume. "There has been an accident on the harbour. Please remain calm and stay inside the stadium as all exits have been closed to accommodate emergency services. I repeat ..."

Jax sprang to his feet and took off at a run. The smell of sulphur increased around him, a sure sign Hades was close. *Stay with me, Arian.* Desperation lent wings to his feet as he charged through the crowd with Odys and Zeus close on his heels. Out the stadium and down La Trobe Street, he ignored the angry shouts from crowd control, dodged the grabbing hands of police officers.

Fear tore at his gut. The Shield of Achilles, release from Purgatory, none of it mattered if Arian wasn't there to share it with him. He had no need of a soul without her. Everything he had to live for lay in the hands of Hades.

His feet pounded against the road surface, the studs on his football boots eating through the surface with each thud. He listened to the crowd. *Bus went off the pier ... driving like a maniac ... no fatalities recorded yet ...* Crossing the tracks, he saw a crowd gathering at the water's edge. Jax searched each face for Arian's.

"What took you so long?"

Jax froze at the sound of Hades' voice. He turned to see the devil sitting on the edge of the pier, invisible to the crowd as he watched the search and rescue. "Where is she, you bastard?"

Hades shrugged. "Down there, somewhere. She's still alive … barely. I won't have to wait much longer. A two for one deal — all in a day's work, I say. A brave girl though. So like her grandmother. She sacrificed her soul for you. She really does love you. When you're ready, I'll be waiting right here for you."

"Screw you," said Jax. "I'm not ready to die."

He kicked off his boots, ripped off his socks, turned and dived into the harbour. The cold water came as a shock and he knew that would knock some points off his life. He schooled his mind to ignore the chill and swam deeper. The pressure squeezed at his lungs.

Eyes stinging from the salt, he peered into the depths. The shadow of the bus loomed below. Against a front windscreen he caught sight of her hair streaming out behind her, her skin almost translucent in the occasional flicker of a dying overhead light.

Ignoring the increasing need to breathe, he swam towards the twisted wreck, looking for a way in. He swam through the back window, forced out by the impact. At least no-one was in there … except Arian.

Her eyes were closed, just as he'd seen her asleep when she was safe and alive. The only clue to her real state was the blue tinge around her mouth. He felt for a pulse. It was there, only faint and erratic. *Hold on, my sweet.*

Lifting her under the arms, he gently tugged her free. His time was running out. He ignored the tearing pain in his lungs, and counted the seconds off in his head to distract his thoughts. Arian's survival was all that mattered.

The twisted metal of the bus and the seats ripped free from the floor slowed his progress. Panic surged through him as Arian's body went slack in his arms and her head fell back. *No! Don't, don't leave me.* Hold on a little longer, he begged silently. With each precious minute that passed, he grew weaker too. The muscles in his arms strained and weakened, his vision blurred as he focused on dragging them both to the surface. Not far to go now. Shapes shimmered in the water from the sunlight above and he fixed his weakening gaze on them like a target.

Dying is not an option, he repeated over and over in his mind. More than anything he wanted to live, to grow babies with Arian, whether on Earth or Mount Olympus, the destination no longer mattered. Getting there did. Calling on his last ounce of strength, he surged towards the surface with Arian clutched to his chest.

Breaking through, he gasped for breath and dragged it deep into his lungs. He tilted Arian's head out of the water and breathed into her mouth. Jax repeated the process — perhaps a half dozen times but it felt like eternity — before the rescue crew reached them and pulled them into the craft. Dizzy from fatigue and lack of oxygen, he allowed them to lay him down but kept a tight grip on Arian's hand as they continued CPR. Just as they reached the pier, he heard her cough and throw up, and thought it was the sweetest sound he'd ever heard.

Transformed and visible once more in his sleek business suit, Hades stood with Zeus and watched as the rescue crew wrapped Jax and Arian in thermal blankets. "Guess you were right, Zeus. I won't be needed here today."

Zeus snorted. "Told you so, but I am curious ..."

Hades cast him a sidelong look but said nothing.

"By taking one, you could have taken the other, yet you took no-one. Why?"

"The boy showed courage. He saved a life when he could have sacrificed his own, just as he did after Troy."

Zeus looked at him, his smile grim. "That's never stopped you before."

Hades shoved his hands in his trouser pockets and shifted his feet. "He's defeated me too many times. I've wanted his soul for a long time. He'd be a great warrior on my security force. Hell is getting a little overcrowded. I've got unionists waging strikes, dodgy politicians causing uproars, internet scammers and hackers ripping off the mob … I could do with some muscle down there to keep them in order." He shrugged. "But his heart is too good and his love for Arian is too strong."

"Again, nothing you haven't faced before."

A sad smile stretched Hades' lips as he smoothed his goatee. "I had a soft spot for Arian's grandmother. She had a good heart too. It almost killed me. It was the closest I ever came to loving and being loved." He shook his head. "There's no place in hell for bleeding hearts. Anyway, if I did take Ajax, I've no doubt that little hellion would come after me to get him back. As much as I love a good fight, Her Highness the Queen is a daunting adversary." He shrugged. "I know when to quit … although … I did reap a little revenge for her stabbing me in the arse with her sword. I had an uncomfortable few moments there. She missed my balls by mere inches." He shuddered. "Don't get too comfortable though, it's not over yet. There are two more souls in your crew on my list and I *will* be waiting for them." He turned to walk away.

"Hades … thanks," said Zeus.

Without looking back, Hades waved a hand. "I must be getting soft in the head. Don't let it get around, will you? You'll spoil my reputation." He melted away into the crowd.

CHAPTER FIFTEEN

There were better ways to spend a Saturday night than under observation in the emergency department at St Vinnie's, wrapped in foil with a drip attached to your arm, Arian decided. The devil had tried to kill her. If he tried again right now, all he'd need to do was put her on a spit and roast her.

"So Craig admitted himself to a drug rehabilitation centre this morning," said Penny. She dropped the small overnight bag she'd packed for Arian on the floor beside the bed. "He confessed to taking hallucinogens, hosting a party with the intention to supply, and is now on suspension until he faces the board. Looks like his career is over. You know what he told the press?"

Arian shook her head. "Something that would cover his arse, I bet."

"It's a classic … wait for it … he reckons the devil made him do it. Now the psyches have him under observation at the clinic."

"Sounds like the perfect place for him. Maybe he'll

stay out of trouble long enough to pull himself together. Am I allowed to go home yet? I really want to get out of here."

"The doctor will be around soon to discharge you and then we'll take you home to the Oakleigh house. Odys and the others are outside, waiting to see you. They're very worried."

"I'm not sure I want to see them right now. I'd rather go back to the apartment and collect my things. I don't want to be away from Paradise for too long, with Hades on the loose again."

"Arian, Jax is beside himself with worry. He's desperate to see you. I said he should wait a little. You were so close to death."

Arian shivered. "Closer than you know." She pulled the blanket to her chest. "I'm not ready to see him. I'm not sure I want to ever again." A lie her mouth spoke and her heart disputed.

"What happened back there? Do you remember anything?" At Arian's hesitation, Penny prompted, "Spit it out, hon. After riding harpies, meeting Zeus and getting up close and personal with a couple of really hunky gods, nothing can shock me anymore."

Arian pushed back the blanket and swung her feet to the floor, more than ready to leave, with or without the doctor's approval. "Lucky *you* never met Hades then."

Penny gasped, and then rattled off like an express train. "Are you serious? Okay, that worked. I'd be speechless but I need to know what the hell went down yesterday. Hades, as in the devil? You saying he had something to do with the crash? What were you doing on the bus anyway?"

"He was in love with Gran, killed Grandad, corrupted

Craig, and was intentionally trying to steal Jax's soul. I wanted answers or revenge, whichever was easiest to extract from his rotten arse." Arian rubbed at the ache in her ribs. "Hades drove the bus into the harbour. A deliberate act meant to kill me and Jax." Anger warmed her chilled bones.

For once, Penny had no comeback. Her eyes grew wide and she muttered, "Shit."

"That's putting it mildly. So here's my dilemma ..." Arian slipped her feet into her shoes, picked up the overnight bag and dropped it on the bed, wincing as the muscles in her body protested. "Jax only needs me to keep him alive and free him from Purgatory. If I stick around, Hades will continue to try and kill one or both of us. If I die, Jax dies."

"Zeus will never allow it. Jax *loves* you, Arian."

"How can he?" Arian turned to her friend tired, sore, defeated. "He doesn't even know me."

Penny put out her hands and held Arian's. "He knows enough to jump off a pier to save you from a sinking bus, to breathe life into your lungs when his own is fading. He's out there now looking like death warmed up in a microwave because he's so worried about losing you."

Arian stamped her foot, tears brimming her eyes. "*Of course*, he's worried about losing me. *Not* because he loves me but because he'll *die* without me." Each word leapt from her lips, emphasised with anger, hurt and disappointment. And with each one, she felt her heart shatter. "I picked me another dickhead, only this one thinks he's a god."

"At least listen to what he has to say?" Penny begged. "You're not thinking clearly ..."

Arian hauled the clean clothing Penny had brought out of the bag, stripped off the hospital gown and dressed in the comfort of her own clothes. She wrapped the too-long sleeves of her favourite sweater around her hands and clenched her fists, jamming them cross-armed into her armpits. The cold no longer came from her dip in the harbour, it came from her heart.

"Actually, I *am* thinking clearly — for the first time since I snorted ouzo up my nose in Mykonos and had sex with a man who thinks he's a Greek god. Get me out of here, Penny. Now."

"Why am I still alive?" roared Jax a week later in the vault below the house in Oakleigh. "End it. I have nothing more to live for."

The Shield of Achilles continued to glow and turn in the protective case, the only sound the hum of the magic that kept it secure. Next to it, his sword taunted him from its sheath.

"Give me my sword that I may fall upon it again." He struck the invisible case with his fist and the force threw him back, landing him on his arse.

Odys sighed. "How many times are you going to do that before you learn?"

Jax flexed his fist, his knuckles red and swollen. "Did you bring me a drink or are you just going to stand there and watch?"

Odys whistled through his teeth. "Grouchy bastard, aren't you? How long are you going to stay drunk until you sober up and go in search of Arian?"

"What for? She has no need of me and I no need of her."

"Well, that's bullcrap. I hear you moaning into your pillow at night." He poured himself a shot of Zeus' brew and took his time drinking it, all the time watching his friend punch the force field, get thrown back and land on his tush. After the fifth time, the skin on Jax's knuckles split and bled, and Odys pushed away from the wall he leaned on. "Zeus has granted you one more chance, Jax. Don't waste it beating yourself up over what happened with Hades."

Jax wiped the blood off onto his jeans. "What use is a chance when I can't see her, feel her, hear her thoughts? How will I reach her? The path to Paradise has been sealed off, the whole planet in lockdown while they rebuild. She doesn't want anything more to do with me." He sank to the floor, elbows resting on his knees as he raked impatient hands through his hair. "Penny won't even talk to me, she ignores my calls."

Odys sat next to his friend and rested his head against the cool wall. "I hear ya. She's not saying much to me either. Helen tried too, even Ermioni, but Penny's mouth stays tighter than a virgin's chastity belt. We're not quitters, Ajax, we're warriors, and we fight for what we want."

Zeus joined them in the vault. "Are you through punishing yourself, young Ajax? Get Helen to patch those knuckles for you."

Jax flexed his fingers and winced. "I'm fine."

The great god glared down at him. "You are a lot of things, my son. Arrogant, stubborn, brave and defiant, but *fine* you are not. Stand up, and go clean yourself up. The harpies are waiting."

Jax squinted up at him, an alcohol-induced headache beginning to thump behind his eyes. "Harpies? Why?"

"I'm sending you on a mission. You have a couple of hours to prepare. Use them wisely." He snapped his fingers and disappeared as quickly as he'd arrived.

As much as Arian loved Paradise, the void in her heart could never be filled, yet every day she rose from her bed and served her people. Paradise prospered and grew, wiping out all traces of the evil Hades had brought there.

Penny, bless her, had spent three long weeks trying to cheer her up, visiting the villages with her to bless the new and reborns. Now even Penny had gone home and the emptiness lingered. She had grown to love her people without question, but the hollowness she felt grew daily, the ache of being incomplete.

"You are sad, Your Highness. Are you not happy with us here in Paradise?"

"No, no, Rhonwen, I love it here. The peace and serenity, the call of the birds, it's all very beautiful." Arian smiled wistfully.

"But?"

"Tell me, Rhonwen, how is it I pine for a man who is a traitor and a liar?" She watched through the window as a bird swooped in from the horizon. Electra was here. Every week she'd stop in with news. How the twins had finally got over the manga stage but now fancied themselves Disney princesses since Arian took control of Paradise. That Penny was looking at opening an ice-cream parlour in Oakleigh and Ermioni had started pre-school. Arian's heart ached. She missed them all terribly. They'd made a great impact on her life in such a short time. Helen with her quiet wisdom, Odys with his wit, dear little Ermioni with her sticky fingers and sloppy cheek kisses, and Jax … oh God, how she missed him.

Electra circled and dipped against the setting sun and Arian caught sight of a figure on her back, sitting tall with all the proud posture of a chieftain. Her heart skipped a beat and lodged in her throat as Electra swooped down in a graceful landing.

She turned away. Even if her eyes hadn't seen him, her heart and soul would recognise him anywhere. She held a hand tight against her churning stomach as Jax slipped from Electra's back. Minutes later, he was led inside by a ring of faeries, their hearts all aflutter over his handsomeness.

"Arian ..."

Jax's voice washed over her like warm chocolate, threatening to melt the ice around her heart. She made a fist against her chest to stem the pain that rose there. He was here but she couldn't — wouldn't — have him. They were worlds apart. She turned from the window with the intention of telling him so, and stopped.

Rising from the sea in those oh-so-hot bathers, Jax was pure Man-god. In full *panoply*, he was every inch a warrior, from the top of his helmet to the leather of his roped sandals. The Shield of Achilles shone brightly, carried on his left arm, held across his muscle *cuirass* with fierce pride. The strong arms that had hauled her from the bottom of Victoria Harbour and lifted her into the lifeboat were bare in the sleeveless *chitoniskos.* Her glance fell on his sword, sheathed firmly at his side.

"Synchoriseme, xechase, s'agapo panta," he said quietly.

Forgive, forget, love always. Arian wrapped her arms around her waist trying to still the butterflies. Ajax stood before her, all trace of Jax Polemistis the relaxed holidaymaker in Mykonos gone, the tense Greek lawyer from Oakleigh eradicated, and in his place a legendary — mythical — soldier, brave enough to lay down his life for honour.

Jax stood tall and tense, his features set in stone, only his eyes betrayed his feelings. Regret, remorse, shame. His hand fisted the gilt handle of his sword, knuckles white, as if he were ready to draw it and fall on it at her command. A command she had no wish to give.

"You used me, Ajax Polemistis. From the first time we met on Paradise Beach right until the showdown with Craig at that football match."

"No." His eyes focused on a spot above her head, all proud warrior.

"Yes. Your mate Hades was happy to put it all in perspective for me. First Zeus handpicked me — Arianrhod, Restorer of Souls, descendant of the Queen of the Faeries."

"No." He stiffened, back ramrod straight, as she stepped into his personal space.

"Oh, you had me fooled. Those glimpses of Paradise in your kiss, that little trick when I choked on the ouzo. What did you spike my drink with?"

"I never spiked your drink. Hades was there that night at the bar in Mykonos. He served you the Greek Tigers."

Arian glared at him. "The trip to the cove and what happened in the hotel room after … all manipulation because you knew I would become the Faerie Queen who could give you back your soul."

He looked at her now, eyes glittering with anger, chin stiff as he stared down the length of his proud Greek nose. "You're wrong, Arian."

She stepped closer and the shield sang with power as it raised a barrier. Arian felt the push and pushed back. "The rules were simple: get the girl, win back the shield Zeus used as a bargaining tool, and he'd give you back your soul and your honour—free you from Purgatory." She reached up and flicked her forefinger off her thumb against the furrows of his frown. "Which one did you want more, Ajax the Great?" she mocked. "Your soul or your possessions?"

"I want you." Still he clung to his sword and shield.

"No, you want it all. You want everything." Arian turned to walk away.

With a roar that shook the walls of the castle, Jax tossed aside the shield. It spun across the room, an overgrown frisbee whistling through the air. Arian made to step around him. Jax's hand on her arm stopped her short.

"Let me explain," he growled.

She looked at the fingers that circled her bicep, strong, long and wide. Fingers that had the power to hurt her — he was angry enough to — yet he only applied enough pressure to hold her still. She felt the strength in his hands, the weight of it he carried in his wide-legged stance, the restraint he maintained with apparent ease, despite the storm brewing in his eyes.

He dropped his hand from her arm, and reached for the

leather straps that secured his breastplate. "You are right. I was sent to find you. You are wrong about the motive."

Arian watched in fascination as he stripped away his armour. Carelessly, he tossed the breastplate on the low couch that faced the two chairs, followed by the golden greaves from his shins, until all that remained was his sword and linen *chitoniskos*. Her gaze was drawn to his powerful legs, all bronzed muscle below the shortened tunic. Anger momentarily gave way to admiration for this beautiful, brave warrior who'd stolen her heart then stomped all over it in greed for possession. She tore her eyes away from the body she'd worshipped with hers.

"I no longer care."

"I do." He walked towards her, stopping when she took a step back. "When I met you on the beach, I knew I wanted more than just to protect you. You touched a part of my heart frozen for too long, but still I harboured a distrust of women. The more time I spent with you, the deeper I fell, the less I could resist you. Yes, I wanted my soul, my release from Purgatory, but I began to need you more. I'd fought for the honour of the shield only to lose it because of a spiteful misdeed. A mistake that would cost me my life, whether I took it myself or in a form of punishment from the Greek army whose sheep I'd slaughtered."

He reached out to touch her face. For a moment, she sank into the warmth of his palm, her heart aching, then she pulled away from his touch and he dropped his hand to his side.

"The night you choked on the ouzo, I felt my soul being ripped away when I thought you were going to die. Hades had used a strong potion, not enough to kill me but you … he could have killed you." Jax pulled off his helmet and it fell against the discarded breastplate with a clang. Raking a hand impatiently through his hair, he looked Arian in the eyes. "Then later, I kissed you and I knew ..."

Arian stepped closer and he held out his hands. She let hers hang at her sides while her heart pounded at the raw need in his eyes. She couldn't be drawn under his spell until she knew the truth.

"You are more than a means of bringing me back to life. You *are* my life." He removed the sheath from around his waist that held his sword, knelt at her feet, head down and offered it up to her with both hands. "Arian, my queen and keeper of my heart, for you I surrender my sword and the Shield of Achilles, in return for your forgiveness and eternal love."

Arian swallowed the lump in her throat and squeezed her eyes shut against the tears that stung her lids. "What does that mean?" she whispered.

He raised his head, his love for her a glow on his face. "It means I sacrifice my immortality, my place in Zeus' army, to spend the rest of my days in Paradise with you, until we die of old age and seek the shores of eternity together."

"You'd do that?"

"In a heartbeat."

She cupped his face between her palms, his beard soft against her skin, and drew him to his feet. "Then I accept your apology."

Later, Arian lay with her head pillowed on Jax's chest, his heartbeat still unsteady in her ear. Their coming together had been wild, uncontrolled and desperate. Skin on skin wasn't close enough as they'd tasted and teased, devoured and adored. His *chitoniskos* lay on top of her discarded robes, the only thing saving it from ruin during removal was that it held together with safety pins—pins now bent out of shape.

"I love you, Arian." His voice rumbled beneath her and the hand that held hers squeezed her fingers tightly.

Arian kissed his chest then looked up to find him watching her. His arm around her waist drew her closer still. "I love you, Jax."

"When you disappeared from the stadium … the accident … I thought I'd lost you. Were it not for Zeus' potion, I might not have had the strength in me to save you."

"Sshh …" Arian wriggled her hand from his and put a finger to his lips.

He kissed the tip. "Then you ran away ..."

"Hades fed me lies so damn believable they made perfect sense. I thought he would come after you again as long as I was around. Jax, if I lost you ..."

"I know." He tipped her face to his and kissed her long and hard.

Breathless, she traced the hard plain of his abdomen, across his hip and down those strong thighs. She loved the feel of him, the dip and rise of his muscles, the firmness of his hold and the heart that beat strong and hard in his chest.

"Are we truly free from him now?"

"Yes, he won't come for us again. This time he'll keep

his promise. Who knew he had a heart, black as it is? We have your gran to thank for that. Looks like she had a thing for bad boys," he teased as his fingers played up the length of her spine. "I can be a bad boy too."

"I am my gran's progeny, and Queen of the Faeries too. I might have to punish you for your misdeeds." She rolled on top of him, aligning their bodies for a fit they already knew was perfect.

"I like your idea of punishment," Jax murmured. His hands stroked across her bottom as he hitched her closer.

She arched away a little, long enough to stroke his length as it pressed between them, smiling as he moaned his pleasure. Then she began a rhythm he couldn't ignore, kissed his lips tenderly and swallowed his whispered words of adoration. As she guided him home, she lifted her head and said, "Jax … will you love me forever?"

"Forever and beyond."

He joined her dance, matching her move for harmonious move. Together they found Paradise.

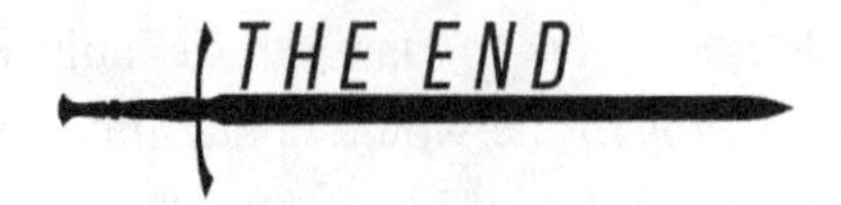

ABOUT THE AUTHOR

FINDING LOVE AND HOPE IN SMALL COUNTRY TOWNS WITH DARK SECRETS.

Juanita escapes the real world by reading and writing Australian Rural Romance novels with elements of suspense, Australian Fantasy Paranormal and Small Town USA stories.

Her romance novels star spirited heroines who give the hero a run for his money before giving in. She creates emotionally engaging worlds steeped in romance, suspense, mystery and intrigue, set in dusty, rural outback Australia and on the NASCAR racetracks of America.

Her small town and Australian rural romances have made the Amazon bestseller and top 100 lists.

Juanita writes mostly contemporary and Australian rural romantic suspense but also likes to dabble in the ponds of fantasy and paranormal with Greek gods brought to life in the 21st century. When she's not writing, Juanita is mother to three boys and has a passion for fast cars and country living.

Author Site: juanitakees.com

Facebook: Juanita-Kees-Author-Page

Twitter: @juanitakees

Goodreads: Juanita_Kees

BookBub: juanita-kees

OTHER BOOKS BY JUANITA KEES

Whispers at Wongan Creek

Secrets at Wongan Creek

Shadows over Wongan Creek

Under Shadow of Doubt

Under the Hood

Under Cover of Dark

Montana Baby

Montana Daughter

Montana Son

Country Whispers

Country Suspense

Country Shadows

Country Darkness

Home to Bindarra Creek

Promise Me Forever